GIRL, 16

five Star FIASCO

Also by Sue Limb

GIRL, 16 five Star Fiasco

SUE LIMB

BLOOMSBURY

LONDON BERLIN NEW YORK

Bloomsbury Publishing, London, Berlin and New York

First published in Great Britain in June 2010 by Bloomsbury Publishing Plc
36 Soho Square, London, W1D 3QY

Text copyright © Sue Limb 2010
The moral right of the author has been asserted

A CIP catalogue record of this book is available from the British Library

ISBN 978 0 7475 9916 6

FSC
Mixed Sources
Product group from well-managed
forests and other controlled sources
Cert no. SGS - COC - 2061
www.fsc.org
© 1996 Forest Stewardship Council

Typeset by Dorchester Typesetting Group Ltd
Printed in Great Britain by Clays Ltd, St Ives plc, Bungay, Suffolk

1 3 5 7 9 10 8 6 4 2

www.bloomsbury.com/childrens
www.suelimbbooks.co.uk

For Alex Meyers

Chapter 1

Jess ran practically all the way to school. There was Fred, looking very tall and gangling in his parka, talking to Mackenzie by the gate.

'Fred!' called Jess. 'Here they are!'

The guys looked towards her, Fred's mysterious grey eyes peering out from his hood as if he was some kind of shy rainforest animal. Jess grinned. Fred was her favourite kind of rainforest animal – after gorillas, of course.

Jess tore open the envelope and pulled them out. 'Ta-ra!' she yelled in a triumphant fanfare. 'Tickets for Chaos, the Dinner Dance of the Century! I can't believe we've organised this! They look really professional, don't they?'

Fred picked one up and peered at it. 'Hmmm,' he pondered. 'They're certainly the best since the tickets to the coliseum in Rome, you know: *Lions, Lemonade and as much Linguine as you can eat . . .*'

'Brilliant!' cried Mackenzie, who was short and curly-haired and bristling with energy. 'Can I have mine? I ordered four.' He ripped some out of Jess's hand.

'Wait, you animal!' yelled Jess. 'You've paid, right?'

'Last week!' Mackenzie assured her, counting out four tickets and pocketing them.

'Wait, wait!' wailed Jess. 'I have to cross you off the list!' She scrabbled around in her schoolbag. There was a cosmetics bag, half an apple core, a spare pair of socks, a copy of a trashy magazine, a few random school books, three pens (two broken), the remains of a cheese sandwich dating back to pre-history, two scrunched-up pieces of paper containing used chewing gum, and half a bottle of cola which had already leaked a tiny pool of dark-brown gunge into the bottom of the bag – but no list.

'Fred!' said Jess urgently. 'I think you had the list – look in your bag!'

Fred continued to admire the ticket. 'We chose the right font,' he murmured. 'I told you Dotum would be better than MS Gothic.'

'Where's the list, Fred?' hissed Jess.

'I haven't got it.' Fred shrugged, handing the ticket back to her. 'You must have left it at home.'

'Urghhh, wait.' Jess remembered something. 'I think there were two lists – or maybe three. There was the list we were working on early last week, because we sold loads of tickets on Tuesday, and then you left that list at home, so on Thursday we made a new list. And I think there was an extra list with a few names on it on Friday.'

'Way to go!' grinned Mackenzie. 'You could be the Queen of Lists!'

Jess smiled faintly, but inside she was panicking. She'd been so sure that Fred had all the lists. But now she wasn't so certain. She'd been concentrating on keeping the cheques safe, and thought she'd handed the lists to Fred.

The bell rang. As they walked into school, Jess grabbed Fred's elbow. 'Listen!' she whispered. 'We can't go dishing out tickets unless we're sure people have paid! And unless we have the lists we can't be sure they've paid or not!'

'We could always make another list,' said Fred. 'I'm in the mood for it. I can feel another list coming on. I'm going to make a list of the people I know who look like characters from history. Starting with that guy in the corner shop who looks like Hitler.'

'Fred, concentrate!' groaned Jess. Fred's kidding around wasn't always appropriate. 'We have to get this right! Otherwise people could gatecrash! We'll have to pretend the tickets aren't available until we've found the list of people who've paid.'

But, of course, they had already let Mackenzie have his.

By break, a crowd had gathered. 'Tickets, tickets!' they were chanting. Pushy Jodie was at the head of the queue – although it wasn't really a queue, more a kind of rugby scrum. Jodie snatched a fistful of tickets from Fred's rather limp, long fingers.

'*Bar, bands, buffet!*' yelled Jodie. 'Excellent! What bands are we having?'

'We haven't quite . . . finalised it yet,' said Jess.

'But there's going to be jazz, right?' asked Ben Jones, his divine face peering over Jodie's shoulder.

'Oh, defo, yes, don't worry!' Jess assured him.

'I ordered six tickets,' said Ben, holding out his hand. 'My mum and dad and my sister and her boyfriend –'

'Who are you taking, then, Ben?' demanded Jodie, turning and staring brazenly into his face.

'Just . . . a friend,' said Ben shyly.

Jess wondered who the lucky girl would be. She had a feeling Ben might bring somebody who didn't go to their school. So many girls at Ashcroft School drooled over him, it was almost a GCSE option. Jess had passed that exam with flying colours – she'd adored him for at least six months, until she'd realised that Fred, though sometimes irritating, was somehow more her sort of guy.

'Fred!' she snapped. 'Don't just stand there! Make another list!'

'OK,' said Fred, getting out his notebook. 'Uhhh, right: tea, milk, pasta, kitchen roll, talcum powder . . .'

'Fred!!???' yelled Jess. 'What kind of list is that?'

'Oh, just my favourite foods,' quipped Fred. 'Talcum powder is great sprinkled on porridge.' He put on his brilliant-but-vacant professor's face, and everybody laughed.

'Fred,' insisted Jess, trying to stay calm, 'make a list of the people who are collecting tickets!'

Fred clicked open his pen. 'What's your name, sir?' he asked Ben.

'He's Santa Claus, and I'm Rudolf!' yelled Mackenzie.

'And I'm Madonna!' added Jodie. 'Hey, stop pushing!'

It was all getting a bit frantic, but Jess could see that, whatever Fred was saying, he was writing down people's real names – more or less. Although his handwriting was so spidery it was going to take them a week to decipher it.

'This is such a great idea, babe,' Jess's best friend, Flora, said into her left ear. Flo squeezed Jess's arm. 'It's going to be such a blast! I'm proud to even know you. Gimme my eight tickets! Mum, Dad, Felicity and Rob, Freya and her horrible Danny, and me and Jack – I must win the prize for buying the most tickets ever!'

'I remember your dad's cheque,' said Jess with a smile. 'It was the biggest cheque I've ever seen!' For a fleeting second, Jess hoped that Flora's dad's cheque was safe with the others in the plastic box at the bottom of her wardrobe (or was it in a big envelope under her bed?). She and Fred must get around to opening a proper bank account for the dinner dance – at £75 for a double ticket, these were big bucks (by Jess's standards, anyway).

'God, it's going to be awesome!' Flora went on, staring dreamily at her tickets. 'Such a brilliant idea to make it a family thing! So the parents don't mind shelling out and everything. If it was just for teenagers

6

I don't think my dad would even let me come.'

'And think of all the money you'll raise for Oxfam!' added Ben.

Jess felt a horrid little lurch of panic: any profit was going to Oxfam, so that made it even more vital to sort out the money side. She suddenly remembered she'd put some cash in her chest of drawers as well – stuffed in a sock or something.

'Are you going to host it, Fred?' asked Jodie, grinning. 'I hope you've got some brilliant gags lined up!'

'We're going to co-host it,' Jess informed Jodie coldly.

'Yeah, the famous Jess'n'Fred double act!' Flora backed her up. 'That's why the tickets are going like hot cakes!'

'No,' said Mackenzie with a strange, almost mischievous grin. 'It's because they're dirt cheap! My dad said he didn't see how you could do a decent dinner dance for the price!'

Jess felt a flare of annoyance. Mackenzie's dad said that, did he? Right! She would single him out for a bit of sarcastic banter during the co-hosting stand-up routine . . .

Walking home after school, Fred and Jess discussed their triumph. At least, it nearly felt like a triumph.

'God!' marvelled Fred. 'All those tickets gone!'

'Except eight,' Jess reminded him.

'Yeah, except eight,' admitted Fred. 'Hey! Why don't we print another hundred?'

For an instant Jess's heart leapt in excitement. Another hundred! More money for Oxfam! And more muns for them to organise all the details, which they must get around to . . .

'Wait, no!' she gasped, suddenly realising something. 'If we print another hundred, there wouldn't be room for everybody in the hall!'

'We could stick a few extra tables out on the pavement,' suggested Fred airily.

'Fred! It's going to be February! Valentine's, remember?'

'We could provide duvets.'

'No, no, don't be stupid. God! It's made me wonder, though – can we fit in the people who have already bought tickets?' A cold wave of anxiety shot up Jess's neck.

'Of course we can!' Fred grinned breezily. 'A hundred is nothing!'

'Maybe we should go to the church hall and have another look at it. A hundred! That's ten tables of ten people each. How big are the tables?'

'Never mind that.' Fred brushed her aside. 'The really important question is: how are we going to host it? In fancy dress?'

Jess was instantly distracted by the idea.

'We could go as animals,' Fred pondered. 'I could be a meerkat. I've always wanted to be a meerkat.'

'You *are* a meerkat,' Jess assured him. 'You have their strange, lost eyes . . . But what would I be?'

'Miss Piggy, of course!' grinned Fred.

Jess hit him with her schoolbag, and as she did so, there was a horrid little crack from inside and some drops of brownish liquid spilled out.

'Oh, that cola!' Jess shuddered. 'I bet it's all over my history book!' She opened her bag and picked out the school books, which were lightly dripping. 'A hankie! A tissue! Give me something to mop them up with!' she pleaded.

'You must know by now that I never carry a hankie,' said Fred. 'That's girls' stuff. I always wipe my nose on the pavement.'

'Oh, Fred!' sighed Jess. 'You're *useless*.'

Chapter 2

It had been a mistake to barge into Mum's bedroom without knocking. She was sitting on the bed, with her laptop on her knees, and as Jess entered, Mum snapped the lid of the laptop shut with a panicky look, as if she'd been caught out.

'Hey, Mum! Why the guilty face? What are you up to?' Jess bounced on to the bed and tried to prise the laptop open. Mum slapped her hand playfully, but hard.

'Stop! It's – a secret!' Mum's face went pink. Hey! Maybe she'd been ordering some kind of surprise treat for Jess! Clothes? DVDs? A day at a spa? A world cruise?

'What kind of secret?' asked Jess, peering into her face. Mum couldn't usually stand up against a really ferocious grilling. 'Is it a nice secret?'

10

Mum looked doubtful. She stuck out her lower lip, sighed and shook her head. 'It could go either way,' she said.

A sudden horrible thought came scorching into Jess's mind. 'You're not looking up illnesses on the internet again, are you?' she demanded. God, that terrible time when Mum thought she had Polymyalgia Rheumatica! ('Polly' for short – it always helps to have a nickname for a nasty illness.)

'No, no,' said Mum hastily. 'I've managed to kick that awful habit.'

'What is it then, Mum? Come on, give me a clue. Maybe I can help.'

'Oh, you certainly can't help.' Mum gave her a very sceptical look. 'Although you could ruin it.'

'Ruin it?' Eagerly Jess pounced on this hint. She could ruin it! What could she ruin? Well, almost anything. The world cruise would be top of her list of things to ruin, of course. What had she most recently ruined? Oh God, the non-stick frying pan – by scraping at it with a metal spoon! 'Are you ordering a replacement non-stick frying pan?' enquired Jess anxiously, because at the height of the ruined frying pan row she had recklessly offered to pay for a new one.

Mum threw back her head and laughed. 'Oh, don't

worry about *that*,' she said, beginning to make a move. 'Come on! Let's go and help Granny with supper.'

'No!' roared Jess, capturing her with a well-aimed rugby tackle. 'Unless you tell me what it is, I shall go down the leisure centre and get into a fight! I'll run away from home and live in a cardboard box with street people! I'll marry a fish!'

'Well, you'll obviously do most of those things anyway,' said Mum, giving up the struggle to escape and going limp. 'Oh, all right. *If* I tell you – and it's a big if . . .'

'Yes? Yes? What?'

'You must promise not to breathe a word to anybody.'

'I promise!' said Jess. 'I really mean it! My lips are zipped!'

Mum gave her a serious, stern look. '*Really*, Jess. It's . . . a delicate subject.'

Surgery! She was going to have a facelift!

'Sure!' agreed Jess, breathless with excitement. Maybe if Mum had a facelift she would look more favourably on Jess's plans for a boob job.

'OK, then.' Mum gave her a doubtful look and flipped open her laptop. 'I'm thinking of . . . well, there's this online dating thing.'

Jess's heart gave a crazy somersault. The facelift went hurtling off into cyberspace. The boob job drooped out of sight. The world cruise sailed away off the map.

'Dating?' Jess gasped. Her mum gestured towards the screen. A gallery of men stared out at them. Somehow they all looked shabby and desperate, as if they'd been floating on a life raft in the Pacific and had to eat their own feet to survive.

'This is what's available within twenty miles of here,' said Mum with a sigh, 'between the ages of thirty and fifty.'

'That's quite a big age range,' Jess pondered. 'I mean, thirty is, like, a toy boy, Mum.' When it came to toy boys, Jess's mum had a bit of history. There had been her Japanese pupil with the glossy shoes, Mr Nishizawa. Jess shuddered at the ghastly memories of this affair, particularly the time when Mr N had come out into the back garden just at the moment when Jess had been driven, by a terrible bathroom crisis, to pee behind a bush.

'Thirty is fine,' Mum insisted firmly. 'I'm not old enough biologically to be the mother of a thirty-year-old.'

'OK, OK,' Jess agreed hastily. 'But, Mum! Fifty is way too old.'

'Madonna is fifty,' Mum reminded her. 'And more to the point, so are Pierce Brosnan, Denzel Washington, Mel Gibson, Kevin Costner . . . Fifty is nothing, these days.'

Jess stared at the photos on the screen. The contrast with Mel and Denzel could not be more depressing. Several of these guys had horrible thick beards, not stylish goatees. There was one called Adrian who had a beard so big you could have built a tree house in it and thrown a party.

'God, Mum,' said Jess, 'these guys all look like losers.'

'You should never judge people by their looks,' Mum argued, although she sounded a little half-hearted about it. Her weakness for the famously ugly Pierce, Denzel, Mel, etc. was well known.

Jess sighed and stared at the candidates, all smiling awkwardly in the manner of serial killers. OK, they looked unpromising. But if one of them turned out to be even vaguely tolerable, it meant that Mum might come to the dinner dance after all. She had so far sternly refused, on the grounds that Jess might be traumatised by the sight of her mother dancing by

14

herself. There's something really weird about parents dancing. That was why Chaos was going to be a family event – so all the teenagers could see their parents dance, feel the fear, eat their own fists, pee themselves laughing and get over it.

'And the fact is, Jess, I've already made arrangements to see one of these chaps.'

'Which? Which?' demanded Jess eagerly.

'You'll see,' said Mum, shutting her laptop with a mysterious smile. 'Now let's help Granny with the supper – and don't breathe a word to her about this, OK?'

Granny had made burgers, and to placate the gods of dieting, she'd done oven-baked wedges of butternut squash instead of chips, plus a salad.

'There's the ketchup,' said Granny, helpfully placing it beside Jess's glass (water, not cola: so saintly!).

Mum was messing about, struggling to open a bottle of wine for herself and Granny. Jess sighed. Why was their corkscrew so primitive? Flora's dad had a state-of-the-art corkscrew that worked on compressed air or something.

'Delicious, Granny!' drooled Jess, lacing the burger with a bloodbath of ketchup. 'You're a star!

And I hope there's nothing chocolatey for pud!'
Actually, this was not quite true – Jess was secretly
hoping Granny had prepared some evil concoction
involving three different types of choc. Jess had made
a new year's resolution about having chocolate only
twice a month. It would be torment, but her skin and
her waistline would thank her.

'No, dear, I remembered your new year's resolution,' said Granny firmly, 'so I just stewed a few pears,
and instead of cream there's low-fat yogurt.' Trying
to maintain a cheery smile at this dire news, Jess got
stuck into her burger. 'How was school today?' asked
Granny.

'Oh, it was brilliant – I gave the tickets to everybody who'd put their name down for Chaos, and they
were all thrilled.'

'What's Chaos again?' asked Granny, frowning
slightly.

'It's the dinner dance, remember, Granny? Fred
and I are organising it in aid of Oxfam.'

'When is this?' said Granny vaguely, but you could
see she was really thinking about the pepper grinder,
which had stopped working properly and instead was
depositing huge rocky grains of fiery pepper on to
the defenceless burgers.

'Valentine's!' said Jess happily.

'Where are you having it?' asked Granny, dismantling the pepper mill with a preoccupied air.

'St Mark's Church Hall!' announced Jess. 'Fred's dad booked it for us, and he's going to run the bar.'

'That was kind of him,' said Mum, pouring two glasses of wine. 'I hope he's got everything under control.'

'Oh yes, Mum, don't worry – we've got everything under control and it's going to be fine!' Jess assured her cheerily.

This wasn't strictly true, either. Although Fred's dad had indeed done the booking for the hall and agreed to run the bar, all the other details – the food, the music, everything, in fact – were being organised by Jess and Fred. Jess had spent nine hours designing the most stylish tickets in the world, but, she thought, with a niggle of anxiety, they really *must* get round to sorting out the rest of it – soon.

Chapter 3

Jess and Fred dived into the Dolphin Cafe after school. It was one of those rainy afternoons when the windows steamed up cosily and the music and voices became a kind of warm blur.

'Where's Her Royal Highness?' asked Fred, as they squeezed into the corner under the stairs – not the best table in the place, but it was all that was available.

'Who?' Jess was baffled.

'Flora, Prom Queen of Ashcroft School,' said Fred in a pompous voice. 'She leaves a trail of broken hearts . . .' His voice sank to a melodramatic whisper. '. . . Pavements, where she walks, turn to marshmallow . . . Bald old men grow hair again when she passes by . . . Mad dogs stop growling and start to recite lines of poetry . . .'

Jess frowned. OK, Flora was amazingly beautiful, but it wasn't Fred's job to say so. At Kate Jackson's party last weekend Flora had been wearing a drop-dead-gorgeous plum satin boned-corset dress with a massive bow at the back – very Hollywood and glitzy. Jess had tormented herself for most of the evening trying to see if Fred was ogling Flora. Shooting side-long glances at your boyfriend to see if he's shooting sidelong glances at your hot best friend is kind of exhausting. Maybe Sidelong Glances should become an Olympic event. Once upon a time Flora had had the hots for Fred, but, Jess told herself sternly, it would be a big mistake to sound jealous and stressy.

'Shut up about Flora being so goddam beautiful and sexy!' snapped Jess, drops of stressy spit flying out of her mouth and landing on Fred's sleeve.

'No need to drown me!' Fred pulled a silly face as if the spit was some kind of toxic chemical and wiped his sleeve on his trousers.

'Well, ordinary girls like me, who look like a camel's bum, get a bit fed up with all that Flora Is A Goddess stuff.' Jess tried hard to moderate her tone into something sensible and calm: she knew she sounded majorly stupid.

'There's no need to feel jealous of Flora.' Fred

had started to look a bit bored.

'I'm not jealous of her!' retorted Jess jealously.

'I don't go for the tall blonde type, for a start,' Fred explained patiently. 'Flora's legs are like sticks, that blonde hair is such a cliché, and, let's face it, she's a ditzy airhead who thinks that Penzance is in France.'

'She does not!' OK, when Fred put on his Flora Is A Goddess act it was irritating, but to say mean things about Flora was totally wrong and unaccept-able. 'Ditzy?' screeched Jess. 'An airhead? Uhh, isn't this the same Flora who gets straight As, beating both you and me in every subject including English?'

Fred shrugged and tried to look charming and irresponsible. 'I'll never mention Flora again,' he promised. 'Except when discussing the flora and fauna of Australia, of course.'

Jess stirred some sugar into her coffee – always a bad sign. When things were a bit dodgy, a spoonful of sugar seemed comforting, although afterwards she was sure she could actually feel it attacking her teeth and pumping up her waistline flab.

'Well, anyway,' she sighed, trying to settle down into normal conversation and beginning to feel she'd sounded stupid and hysterical, 'Flora's with Prince Charming.'

'What?'

'You know – Jack Stevens!'

Flora and Jack had got together last term when they were in the school production of Shakespeare's *Twelfth Night*. Flora had been delighted to discover that Jack's brooding scowl was just a cosmetic choice, a bit like conditioner, and she insisted that underneath it all he was as soft as a doughnut and so, *so* funny. He was in the sixth form and his family had taken Flora skiing at Christmas, so he scored maximum points on the Index of Cool.

'Oh, *him*,' said Fred.

'What do you mean, *him*?' Jess asked indignantly.

Fred shrugged.

'But you sounded sneery.'

'No I didn't. I hardly know the prat.'

'He's not a prat! Fred, you're jealous! Jack's a star! And what's more, he's totally posh! His dad owns a printworks and Flora says their house is like something out of Jane Austen! Plus they've got a holiday home by the sea somewhere – on some cliffs – and a boat.'

'Oh dear, I seem to have underrated him,' said Fred ironically. 'I may just have to lie down and let him walk all over me!'

21

'He won't want to set foot on you!' Jess informed him with a teasing smile. 'He'd ruin his shoes!'

She was beginning to feel a tad better. Enjoying witty banter with Fred had been the best thing in her life for months, even if sometimes, when Fred was behaving like an idiot, he got on her nerves a bit.

'On a different subject entirely . . . guess what?' Fred's eyes were dancing. Some joke was coming, for sure.

'What?'

'My mum got a postcard from some old friend of hers – she's on holiday in Italy, and apparently there's a church there dedicated to St Fred.'

'St *Fred*? No way!'

'Well, I think he's called St Fredianus or something.'

'Fredianus? Don't be gross! Although, you know, it kind of suits you. In fact, I think I'll call you that from now on.' Jess was back in tune with Fred now, bubbling along nicely. 'How is your mum, by the way?' Jess loved Fred's mum, who was always very sweet to her. She'd even baked Jess's favourite cheese scones last time she was at Fred's for an *X File* orgy.

'Oh, she's OK,' sighed Fred. 'She's getting a crush on Simon Cowell, though – I recognise the signs. I hope she's not going to start stalking him or entering

Britain's Got Talent or something. Obviously it would be more glamorous to have divorced parents, but I'm not sure I could stand Simon Cowell as a stepdad.'

'But think of the sports car and the apartment in LA!' said Jess. 'If you don't want him as a stepdad, I'll give him a good home. He can't be any worse than some of the guys my mum is dating.'

'Your mum is dating?' Fred's eyes got bigger and bigger until the whites showed all the way round.

'Oops! I wasn't supposed to mention that! Oh God! I don't like to talk about it, of course, because it's so very traumatic for me, her only daughter, but yes, Mum has joined an online dating agency. Don't laugh! And don't breathe a word to anybody!'

'Online dating?' repeated Fred, his eyebrows sky high. 'Your *mum*?'

'Yeah, God, it's so unbelievably gross!' Jess shuddered. 'There are these guys – they're in her checkout basket or something, anyway, you can see their photos and read their biogs and whatever, and they literally all look like terrorists or paedos. It's horrendous.'

'So who's her first victim?'

'Well, I hope it's not Mum who's going to be the victim – I'm getting so nervous about her, it's ridiculous. Talk about role reversal! I'll be waiting up till she gets back and texting her every five minutes!'

'And if she gets in after midnight,' suggested Fred satirically, 'you should tell her she's been grounded.'

At this point the cafe door opened and Jess heard somebody call her name. It was Flora, clinging picturesquely to the sleeve of Jack Stevens.

'Oh God, here come Flora and Jack,' whispered Jess, while eagerly waving them over towards the two empty chairs at their table. 'Fred Parsons, if you say one word out of line, I'll make you wish you'd never been born.'

Chapter 4

'Hi, Parsnip!' This was Jack's greeting to Fred.

'Ah, it's the prince of darkness!' This was Fred's reply. But he also managed a grin, so Jess was satisfied. It was a sly, sarcastic grin, but then that was Fred's usual.

'I'll get a hot choc,' said Flora. 'What would you like, Jack?'

'Red Fusion,' drawled Jack, taking off his flying jacket. 'Hot in here, huh?' He tossed back his hair but a few strands fell over his face. Then he smoothed down the collar of his shirt and smiled at Jess. This was something Fred never did. Not the smiling – the smoothing. Fred's shirt often had one side of the collar down and one poking up. Somehow this gave him the air of a chihuahua who had just woken up from a deep sleep.

'So, how are my favourite comedy writers?' Jack included Fred in his smile. It swept across the table like a warm wind from the south. His teeth were big and white and expensive-looking. He had big rubbery expensive-looking lips, too. But, actually, he always seemed really nice. It wasn't his fault he was rich.

'We're stuck with our hosting script for Chaos,' Jess told him. 'I think we may have peaked too soon. Sixteen is way too young to feel you're on the down-hill slope.'

'That show you did at Christmas was amazing,' said Jack. 'You're going to be the next big thing. French and Saunders, Mitchell and Webb, Horne and Corden . . . Jordan and Parsons.'

'Jordan and Parsons doesn't sound right,' Jess mused.

'It's the Parsons that's the problem.' Jack looked teasingly across at Fred, who was leaning back in his chair and biting his nails in a way that was far from attractive. 'You should change your name to André. Jordan and André.'

'They're history,' said Jess. 'Anyway, people are always pointing out that I'm too flat-chested to live up to my name.' At this point Jack looked at her boobs – well, she'd almost issued an invitation. Jess

26

regretted it and blushed. No way did she ever want Jack to fancy her – except in the kind of louche, secret way you always want your best friend's boyfriend to fancy you.

'Big boobs are overrated,' said Jack. 'Although they would look great on Fred. Hey, bro! Get yourself some implants. That would do wonders for the comedy.'

'I'll get implants,' said Fred, 'if you get a brain transplant.' It wasn't Fred's best quip ever. By his standards, it was lame and sounded a bit desperate. Jess rushed to obliterate it.

'God, I'd love a brain transplant!' she gushed. 'I'd have Stephen Fry's! Hey, maybe Fry would be a good name for you, Fred!' Fred gave her the kind of look that a snake gives a mouse – kind of sinister, from below half-closed lids. 'Fred Fry!' Jess blundered on. Why was Fred being so unhelpful? 'Although Fred told me just now that there's an Italian saint called Fredianus.'

'Brilliant!' Jack exploded with laughter and slapped his thigh. 'Fredianus it is, buddy!' Fred shot Jess a look that would have curdled custard. At this point, luckily, Flora arrived with the drinks.

'Guess what!' she bubbled excitedly, shaking back

her blonde hair and ripping off her gilet. 'Jack's mum and dad are going to their beach house the weekend after next! We're all invited! There's a kind of dorm upstairs with about ten beds so loads of us can come! Jack's brother George is at uni and some of his mates are coming! You *can* both come, can't you? It'll be brilliant!'

'I'm, uh, not sure . . .' Fred pulled a strange ungracious face and rubbed his nose. 'Won't we be busy organising the Chaos thing?' He looked at Jess and raised his eyebrows. 'It'll be coming up to the fourteenth the weekend after, I think. Must be, yeah.' Jess felt slightly sick for a moment. Somehow she had imagined that there were weeks and weeks before the dinner dance, even though she'd designed the tickets herself and, of course, knew very well that it was to be on the 14th February. But the invite to the weekend by the sea was too good to refuse.

'Of course we're coming, Flo!' she yelled. 'It'll be absolutely brilliant! Thanks so much! We can get the organising all done before we go!'

'Of course, the Aged Parents will be around,' said Jack with a sigh, 'so a total orgy is out of the question.'

'Never mind!' Jess could see Fred was a bit iffy

about the trip. He was leaning his head on his hand and pulling his lips about in an unattractive way. Maybe he felt inadequate, lip-wise – Jack's lips were like a sofa; Fred's were thin and nervy – but Jess wished he would stop doing it. 'It sounds just awesome!' she went on fervently. 'Fred and I had the best time at my dad's down in St Ives last summer!'

'Except now it's midwinter,' Fred pointed out, making it sound like some kind of terrible curse.

'Maybe we'll get snowed in!' suggested Flora, her eyes sparkling at the thought. 'So romantic!'

'Yeah,' agreed Jack. 'It's an amazing sight – the beach covered in snow. Weird!'

'Can you actually see the beach from your house?' asked Jess.

'Yeah, it's right on top of a cliff, and there's a path that goes down to this little cove.'

'Oh my God!' screamed Jess in ecstasy. 'It sounds deee-vine!' She clutched her cheeks to prevent her face from flying apart with sheer excitement.

'Yeah, it's good,' Jack conceded modestly. 'Last year, George – that's my bro who's at uni – made a Loch Ness Monster suit and went in the sea. This family arrived on the beach, yeah? With little kids and stuff. And George went swimming past with this,

29

like, dinosaur neck thing poking out of the water. The kids went mental! We were hiding in the dunes. I laughed so much I nearly puked.'

'I can't wait! I so adore the sea!' Flora's eyes were already a kind of aquamarine at the thought. Fred's, however, remained grey and his face seemed somehow veiled in mist. Suddenly he got to his feet.

'Excuse me, guys,' he said, his lanky body kind of wobbling, a bit like an embarrassed giraffe saying goodbye to its favourite tree. 'I gotta go – Mackenzie asked me to drop by his place to talk about some bands we might get for Chaos.'

He gave a sort of awkward nod, and was gone – without even looking at Jess! They'd been planning to walk home together! They always did after school! He hadn't even given her any eye contact! Jess felt as if she'd been stabbed terribly in the guts, but somehow she had to hide her horrible wound and be bubbly and vivacious as usual. If Fred had behaved badly, that wasn't Jack's fault. Or Flora's. He was being an idiot.

'Fredianus,' said Jack fondly, watching Fred leave the cafe with just the tiniest hint of a slam. 'What a legend!'

They chatted for a bit longer, but Jess's thoughts

were elsewhere: with Fred. She didn't quite believe that excuse about organising the music for Chaos. She had a feeling Fred just wanted to escape for some reason. He could be a moody beast at times – the best thing to do was ignore him.

Jess ignored him all the way home, even though he wasn't technically present. She was on her own. Flora and Jack had gone off to Flora's, wrapped round each other, because Jack was going to 'help her with her homework' – something, incidentally, Fred never did for Jess. Distracting her from her homework was more his style. Jess spun several revenge fantasies in which Fred pleaded for her to be kind to him, but instead she imperiously dismissed him with a contemptuous flick of her long raven tresses. In reality, Jess's hair was short and spiky. But she was planning to have heavy, thick, glistening hair right down her back one day.

In this way, half an hour was agreeably passed until she arrived home. As she went up the path, the front door opened and Granny came out. She was wearing her faux sheepskin coat and looked rattled.

'Your mother's in there with one of her precious boyfriends off the internet!' snapped Granny. 'I'm going round to Deborah's! She's taken leave of her

31

senses!' Jess assumed this referred to her mum, not Deborah – a friend of Granny's who was about as sane as anybody had ever been, possibly because she spent all her time making and devouring delicious cakes.

At this moment Jess's phone bleeped to indicate a text had arrived. She stopped on the doorstep to check it out – it would be Fred apologising, with any luck. But no. It was from Dad.

HAD A V V BRILL IDEA FOR PROJECT WE CAN DO, it said. **HAVE SENT U EMAIL WITH DETAILS. REPLY ASAP. LUV, DAD, OR, AS I WANT TO BE KNOWN FROM NOW ON, LORD VOLCANO.**

Jess sighed, put her phone away and got out her key. She had the feeling she was being overwhelmed by several kinds of madness.

Chapter 5

As Jess entered the hall, her mum popped out of the sitting room, heading for the kitchen. Seeing Jess, she stalled, looked agitatedly towards the sitting room, flapped her hands to show she wanted to say a thousand important things but must remain silent, then put on her public face.

'Jess!' she said in her public voice – the light-hearted one, which she used whenever they didn't want to mention the corpse on the carpet. 'Hi, darling!' Her mum never called her darling except in emergencies. 'How was school?'

'Delightful, as usual.' At least Jess was determined to keep the conversation normal. 'An endless succession of wonderful treats.'

'Come and meet Ken,' said Mum, a strange expression masking her face, as if she was possessed by a demon. They entered the sitting room and were enveloped by a strange and sickening smell.

A man was sitting on the sofa. The smell could only be coming from him, unless a crocodile had died behind the sofa some days ago and it had somehow escaped their notice. The man was small and dark and, spookily, he seemed to have borrowed the head of a much bigger man. Maybe he had bought it on eBay.

As heads go, it wasn't unpleasant. Basically, it was a low-budget Robert De Niro, with black slicked-back hair, a long hooked Roman nose, bristling eyebrows and a strong stubbly chin – you could see he had to shave about three times a day. He was wearing tracksuit bottoms and a rugby shirt, with a thicket of dark hair sprouting out of the top. He was not so much a possible date as some kind of wildlife park.

On seeing Jess, he got to his feet and extended his hand, his face cracking open to reveal a ragged row of yellow teeth. The handshake was disastrously limp – you'd have got more of a touchy-feely thrill from a dead handbag.

'This is my daughter, Jess,' said Mum faintly. 'Jess, this is Ken.'

'Hi, Ken,' said Jess, trying to hide her deep disgust.

'Hi, Jess.' Ken's voice was unexpectedly deep, dark and sexy. Presumably Mum had seen a flattering photo emphasising the De Niro side of things, been impressed with his telephone voice and then been horrified to be enveloped in his aroma.

I mustn't be prejudiced, thought Jess urgently. *He might be really nice once you get past the smell.*

'Ken was just telling me about his CD collection,' said Mum with an anguished glare. 'He's into classical music.'

'Yes,' said Ken, 'we were discussing the *St Matthew Passion*. Do you like classical music, Jess?'

'I'm afraid I've never really got into it,' said Jess defiantly. 'It makes me feel kind of depressed and Sundayish. Although the theme tune of *The Apprentice* is cool – what's that?'

'Prokofiev!' boomed Ken. For a moment Jess thought he'd sneezed or coughed. Foreign names can be like that. 'Prokofiev's a bit showy for my taste,' Ken went on. 'You can't compare him to the *St Matthew Passion*.'

'What exactly was St Matthew's Passion?' asked Jess. 'Mine is ice cream.'

Ken didn't even register the joke, he just kind of launched himself into a stream of words. 'It's the Passion of Christ, obviously the crucifixion, you know?'

Jess did know – she was planning to crucify Ken in a few minutes' time. In fact, she'd already chosen the exact place on the wall where he would fit in nicely: between Mum's graduation photo and a print of Van Gogh's sunflowers.

'There's nothing to beat the *St Matthew Passion* performed on period instruments,' Ken rolled on. Jess didn't like the term 'period instruments' for reasons she didn't want to go into right now. 'You can't beat the Netherlands Bach Society,' Ken informed them.

He pronounced 'Bach' like 'Bark', making Jess briefly wonder if there was a choir composed entirely of dogs and, if so, whether they could be persuaded to chase Ken down the street and over the horizon, snapping ferociously at the seat of his pants.

'Ton Koopman is my favourite conductor,' Ken went on remorselessly, like a steam roller. 'Although I'm also impressed by Jos van Veldhoven.'

'They sound like footballers.' Jess was trying to head him off while Mum stood helplessly by her side.

There was a split second of silence.

'I was just going to make a cup of tea,' said Mum.

'I can't stand football,' Ken said, and shook his head with a kind of shudder at the mere thought of it.

'We love football, don't we, Mum?' Perhaps this would put Ken off. 'God! Mum just salivates over Wayne Rooney's knees! And I want to have Ronaldo's baby!' Ken looked mystified and revolted.

'Jess wants to be a comedy writer,' explained Mum, with a feeble smile. 'She's occasionally charming but mostly insane, I'm afraid.'

'Comedy. Ah! Ha ha!' Ken produced something clearly intended to be a laugh, but which would have qualified him to sing bass in the Netherlands Bark Society, along with the mastiffs and bloodhounds. 'Comedy, eh, Jess? Good luck! I think you're marvellous!'

Jess retreated towards the door. Though she was committed in a general way to being marvellous, she'd just as soon Ken found her utterly vile, thanks very much.

'Do you like biscuits?' she enquired, trying to sound as un-marvellous as possible. In fact, she delivered the question with a sinister sneer, as if she was planning to slip him a flapjack made of toad's skin.

'Usually I avoid biscuits,' boomed Ken, 'because of the sugar and the wheat, you know – they can make me a bit hyper.'

God help us, thought Jess. *If he's like this now, what will he be like when he's got a couple of chocolate biscuits inside him?*

'But I'm suffering a bit from low blood sugar,' Ken informed them menacingly. 'It often dips at this time in the day.'

'Biscuits it is, then!' cried Mum, and she and Jess ran out to the kitchen together.

Behind them, Ken sat in a horrible silence. If only they had a recording of something played on period instruments! Although Mum owned a CD or two, the CD player had stopped working after an unfortunate accident involving the Christmas tree and a pot of tea.

Mum filled the kettle, staring at a robin on the bird table out in the garden. You could see she was longing to elope with that bird.

'So, how was school?' she asked again, loudly. Their conversation could obviously be overheard in the sitting room, even with the kettle seething quietly towards boiling point (an emotional state quite accurately reflecting Jess's).

'School was fine,' said Jess distractedly. Mum was scribbling something down on a piece of paper. 'History was the best lesson today, because Mrs Fitzherbert had a coughing fit.'

'Oh, good, dear,' said Mum absently. She pushed the note across the table. It read: *For God's sake, get rid of him.* 'And how's Fred?'

Jess grabbed the pencil. *HOW???* she wrote. 'Oh, fine. Fred's organising the music for the dinner dance.'

'Oh, lovely,' said Mum, scribbling again. *Pretend to be ill,* she wrote.

What's that horrible stink? wrote Jess. 'How was your day?' she trilled, in a conversation that was taking place somewhere on another planet.

'Oh, not too bad. Alison's going down with a cold so we must remember to take our vitamin C,' replied Mum. Then she seized the pencil. *I was supposed to go out for a drink with him. Say you've got period pain and then I'll have to stay here.*

At this point the kettle boiled, the tea was made, and Jess cracked open a packet of chocolate biscuits and stole a few of Granny's custard creams.

Lay it on with a trowel, added Mum, with heavy underlining.

They carried the tea tray into the sitting room. Ken was sitting upright like a robot. Jess wondered all over again how such a big head could have been assigned to such a short man. She wasn't against short men in principle – Mackenzie at school, for instance, was cute and cuddly, and so was Tom Cruise, come to that – but Ken had nothing going for him except his possible departure.

'Mum,' Jess faltered, reaching deep into her drama department, 'I feel a bit weird.' She plonked down on to a chair.

'You look pale, darling!' cried the strange false mum who called her darling. 'What is it?'

'Period pain!' gasped Jess, clutching her tummy. If Ken wanted period instruments, that's what he was going to get. 'Oh dear! I think I'm going to faint!'

'Put her head between her knees!' suggested Ken impertinently.

You keep out of it, you stinking weirdo, thought Jess.

'You ought to lie down.' Mum pulled at her arm. 'I'll get a hot water bottle!'

'Shall I help get her upstairs?' Ken cried eagerly, leaping to his feet. What was this? Men usually became uneasy and slunk away furtively at such times.

'No, it's all right!' screamed Mum in alarm. 'This is routine for us. Just pour yourself a cup of tea, I'll be back down in a minute.'

Once safely in Jess's bedroom, a strange madness came over them. Mum's eyes took on a deranged quality.

'Lie down!' she whispered. 'I'll get you a hot water bottle!'

'But, Mum, I'm perfectly OK!' Jess reminded her. 'I haven't really got period pain!'

'Oh my God!' Mum grabbed her hair in a frazzled gesture. 'What planet am I on?'

'Never mind that – what planet is *he* from?' whispered Jess. She burst into a terrible fit of giggling. Mum joined her. They fell on the bed and shook with silent laughter, filling their mouths with parts of the pillow. Eventually Mum dragged herself off the bed and started pulling her clothes tidy.

'Thanks, thanks,' she said. 'I'll go and get rid of him now. If you haven't heard him leave by half past, come down and faint on the floor or be sick over him.'

'I can't just vomit at will, Mum,' Jess informed her. 'Though I admit it would look good on my CV – I could probably get a job in the circus.'

41

'Don't!' Mum looked unhinged for a moment. 'I mustn't laugh! I could go hysterical just like that! I'm right on the edge!' She nerved herself up by the door for a moment, crossed both fingers in a kind of symbolic salute and then left the room.

Jess's phone bleeped again. Another text message! It would be Fred this time, apologising and reporting success in fixing up the band for the dinner dance.

But it was Dad again. **YOU AND I ARE GOING TO STAR IN A GOTHIC HORROR MOVIE. CHECK YR EMAIL AND RING ME ASAP!**

Huh! Little did Dad know that Jess was starring in a Gothic horror movie already – right now, in the privacy of her own home.

Chapter 6

Jess switched on her laptop and found Dad's email. *Good afternoon to my only descendant*, it began. Oh, so he was in one of those moods. *Listen, I've had a terrific idea. Why don't you and I write a story together – one paragraph at a time – and if we sell the film rights, we'll go halves! I've been reading Philip Pullman's* His Dark Materials *and it's totally blown my mind. I've started some dark blue paintings with a kind of Gothic fantasy element, although Phil says they'll never sell. He sends his love, by the way – he's out surfing.* (Phil was Dad's boyfriend. He surfed all year round – he had a state-of-the-art wetsuit. He could afford it, because he had successful boutiques in St Ives, Newquay and Penzance.)

Attached to the email was a document called *Lord of the Wrongs*. Jess's heart sank. She didn't have time for this. She needed to supervise De Niro's departure and call Fred about the band. But she really missed Dad – it was tough, living two hundred miles apart – so she opened the attachment and read on.

Lord Volcano stood at a window of a tall tower overlooking the sea, stroking his beard. The sky was blue. The sea was blue. His beard was blue. No wonder I'm feeling a bit down, *thought Lord V. His beard was growing so, so slowly.* I'm not getting enough protein, *he fretted. It had been a mistake to barbecue all the rats in a one-off Christmas binge. He was waiting for his beard to grow long enough to dangle down to the ground (30 metres, approx). Then his long-lost daughter would surely come and rescue him. Lord Volcano was being held prisoner in the tower by the wicked Sir Filo Pastry, who . . .*

The document stopped abruptly. Dad was such a clueless idiot when it came to computers! He had obviously lost half his document. Unless – wait! Maybe this was where Jess was supposed to pick up the story. She saved a copy and stared at the last sentence, her mind racing, then she started to write.

The wicked Sir Filo Pastry, who . . . was jealous of Lord Volcano's ability to communicate with animals, and

44

jealous, also, of his magic socks.

Meanwhile, far away in the east, Lord Volcano's lovely daughter Messica was also imprisoned, by a wicked witch who lured men to her modest semi-detached hovel in order to steal their thoughts and weave herself a magic cloak from them. Currently Messica was lurking in her room, while downstairs the witch was offering magic potions to a man with an unusually large head which he had slightly over-stuffed with music. Occasionally a few notes of Prokofiev would trickle out of his right ear, and the witch would catch them in a jam jar. But soon she . . .

She whizzed the document back to Dad. This was quite fun after all. Suddenly, she heard the front door open and close. Ken must have gone – unless it was Mum who had gone, leaving Jess alone with Mr Potato Head. The thought made Jess's blood run cold. She tiptoed to her bedroom door and opened it a crack.

'He's gone!' Mum yelled from the hall. 'Oh my God! Quick, where's the air freshener?'

'How come you got as far as a date with that weirdo?' Jess demanded, thundering downstairs. She ran into the sitting room and sniffed. 'It's still there! What *is* that horrendous stink?'

'It's that smell you get when you don't dry your clothes quickly enough,' said Mum. 'You know, if they get left in the washing machine too long or something.'

'But, Mum, how in your wildest dreams could you have imagined Ken might be a good idea for a date?'

'The photo he posted on his page was quite attractive,' said Mum, shaking her head in disbelief. 'I mean, there's nothing actually wrong with his features. In fact, he's quite handsome in a peculiar sort of way.'

'But his head didn't match his body, Mum! We're close to Frankenstein territory here.'

'It wasn't the size of his head that freaked me out,' said Mum, running to the kitchen and rummaging under the sink for the air freshener. 'It was what was inside it. All that stuff about music. I mean, I've nothing against music – it's totally life-enhancing – but he was dangerously obsessed. Ironically, when he mentioned his love of classical music on his biog, I found it reassuring. And he works for a charity. He sounded really interesting and simpatico.'

'Everybody who joins that website should be forced to describe how they smell,' said Jess, as they squirted the sofa.

'But nobody knows how they smell,' argued Mum. 'Anyway, sometimes I don't smell too brilliant myself – like when I've been out in the garden spreading compost about.'

'You do smell good!' insisted Jess. 'You always smell of that sunscreen, even in winter. I'm the one who's rank. Sometimes if I get sweaty I smell just like an onion bhaji.'

'Dad always smelt nice,' said Mum a tad wistfully. 'His aftershave was vetiver.'

'It still is,' said Jess. 'And his skin smells of sunshine.'

'Let's burn one of those scented candles he gave me for Christmas!' suggested Mum tragically. 'It's symbolic. I shall be burning my hopes of some kind of meaningful relationship. Goodbye to men and good riddance.'

'Don't give up, Mum!' Jess began to feel a pep talk was necessary. 'Just because Ken was weird, it doesn't mean they all will be. The next one might be heavenly. Like Frasier or something – see if one of them is a psychiatrist. Let's have another look at the website.' Like some kind of fairy god-daughter, Jess was determined that Mum *would* come to Chaos, the Dinner Dance of the Century, if indeed she and Fred

47

managed to organise it in time.

'I might go online again after supper,' said Mum with a sigh. 'I need to keep my strength up though, or I'll be needing a psychiatrist, big time.'

For supper they had a Jamie Oliver pasta recipe, and felt annoyed that, though Jamie was the right age for Mum's toy boy, he seemed to be happily married. Life was so harsh sometimes.

'What you need, Mum,' suggested Jess, 'is some-body a bit like Jamie Oliver, but with a hint of Barack Obama and maybe a tiny dash of Mel Gibson.'

They were halfway through trying to imagine such a person when Jess's phone rang. This must be Fred, at last!

But it was Flora. 'Hi, Jess!' she trilled. 'We've been planning the weekend at the house by the sea and Jack's shown me loads of photos of it – it's absolutely amazing! I've just emailed you the photos so you can see for yourself! The view from the veranda is liter-ally right down to the sea! And in the sitting room there's this massive fireplace and we're going to have log fires there and do charades and stuff! I so totally can't wait!'

Thank God Flora hadn't said anything about Fred going off like that when they were in the Dolphin

Cafe. Maybe it hadn't seemed odd to her. Jess certainly hoped so. She couldn't resist telling Flora all about Mr Potato Head and Mum's dating, even though she couldn't help feeling that somehow, as usual, Flora's evening had been a lot more entertaining than her own.

Flora had spent the evening with Jack looking at lovely photos of his house by the sea. Jess had spent the evening squirting air freshener around. Where was Fred when she needed a laugh? He was the wittiest boy in Ashcroft School, after all. Should she ring him or wait till he rang? It was so his turn – he'd gone off in a kind of huff. If she left it and he didn't call, it could turn into a nasty little tiff. Jess decided to grasp the nettle. She hated rows, so she went upstairs and called Fred from the privacy of her bedroom.

'Where were you when I needed a laugh, you rat?' she demanded, hoping a faux-jolly approach would work best.

'Doing stuff at Mackenzie's,' replied Fred. He sounded slightly furtive.

'Have you sorted out the band yet?' asked Jess eagerly. Mackenzie was a bit of a show-off, but he did know all the local bands.

'Uh, not exactly,' said Fred shiftily. 'We did ring a couple, but they already had gigs lined up – because it's Valentine's, of course.'

'Oh God!' gasped Jess. 'I hadn't thought of that! Of *course*! But we've got to find somebody.'

'Don't worry,' said Fred nervously. 'There are still loads to try: Frenzy, Goldilocks, The Car Crusher, The Evil Toads . . . How are you getting on organising the buffet?'

'Was I supposed to be organising the buffet?' Jess felt a cold thrill of fear all across her scalp.

'Well, you know how useless I would be at that sort of thing,' said Fred.

'Didn't Jodie say she'd give us a hand?' Jess racked her brains for a reason to be cheerful.

'Have you tasted her beefburgers?' enquired Fred. 'They're like an industrial accident.'

There was a horrid pause, during which Jess began to panic so deeply her hands went dead.

'Never mind,' said Fred. 'If it all goes pear-shaped, we can elope to Vegas.'

This wasn't terribly reassuring.

Chapter 7

While Jess was having breakfast the next day, a text arrived from Flora. BTW, DON'T TELL JODIE ABT BEACH WEEKEND AS SADLY NO ROOM FOR HER. BUT SHE'S TROUBLE ANYWAY SO WHO CARES?

'Oh, Mum,' said Jess with a careful smile, 'by the way, Flora's invited me for a weekend away at Jack's family's place by the sea.'

'Where exactly?' asked Mum in an alert, pouncing kind of way.

'Oh, I'm not sure.' Mum always wanted details, which was irritating. 'Jack's mum and dad are going to be there, though, so it's nothing to worry about.'

'But where is this? How are you going to get there?' Mum was now on Red Alert.

'It might begin with a D . . . Devon? No, ah, Dorset.'

'Dorset!' beamed Granny. 'There was a wonderful

murder there once. They made it look as if this chap had thrown himself off the cliff but, actually, he'd been pushed!'

Mum went pale. Jess silently cursed Granny's ability to whip Mum up into a frenzy of survival anxiety.

'Oh my God, those cliffs!' gasped Mum. 'When was this murder? How horrible!' The weekend in Dorset, which had up till now seemed a heavenly prospect, was acquiring ghastly homicidal overtones.

'It was only in a book, dear,' said Granny soothingly. 'One of Agatha Christie's, I think.'

Mum didn't look at all reassured that the clifftop plunge had only been fictional – after all, sometimes life does imitate art and Jess had always been strongly influenced by literature.

'Who's driving you down to Dorset?' enquired Mum urgently, staring at Jess with panic-stricken eyes. Jess knew she had already imagined the crash site in gory detail. 'It's not Jack, I hope!' One of the really cool things about Jack was that he'd passed his driving test and already had his own car, whereas Fred only had a skateboard.

'I don't know! Maybe! Jack's passed his test and Flora says he's a really safe driver!' Jess was beginning to get hot and bothered. She'd had five hundred versions of this conversation with her mum in the fevered privacy of her mind – she had known it was going to be an issue.

'Flora's hardly a good judge!' snapped Mum. 'Her father thinks he's doing Formula One!'

'Well, if it makes you happy, I'll go by train!' shouted Jess. 'Or bus!'

'It's only because I love you, Jess!' Mum seized her hand, abandoning her cornflakes and giving in to a full-blown panic. Jess knew she had started imagining a train crash, or the bus brakes failing on a long hill running down to the sea.

'I'll walk, then!' she yelled, though she knew even this gesture would not reassure her mother, who sometimes seemed convinced that Jess could be involved in a crash even when lying peacefully in her bed at home. Indeed whenever a plane went low over the house, Mum ran outside and looked up desperately, as if she was planning to catch it if it plummeted down, and to throw it over the fence into the Joneses' next door.

'There's no need to shout,' said Mum, annoyed that her loving gesture had been rejected. 'When is this weekend?'

'Uhhh, I think Flo said the weekend after next.'

Mum's brow clouded with an entirely new and perhaps more realistic anxiety. 'But, Jess, that's the weekend before your dinner dance!' Jess's heart missed a beat.

'I know,' she said, feeling the blood drain from her face but determined to hold steady at this slightly frightening thought.

'Have you organised everything?' demanded Mum.

'Yeah, yeah, don't worry!' Jess had steadfastly refused to let Mum help with the organising – she was determined to prove that she could do it on her own, and though her mum had offered several times to help in any way, Jess felt that having her mother on board would make her look like a loser. Besides, she wanted to prove to her family that she really was organised and capable.

At break Jess nervously shared a chocolate bar with Flora. Already, only three weeks into the new year, she'd violated her new year's resolution several times. But she desperately needed comfort food, because she was beginning to feel horribly uneasy about the chaos of Chaos. She hadn't managed to see Fred yet today, as he'd been late for school and for the first double period they were in different subject groups. And now Fred had gone off to ask Mr Dickson something about Chess Club.

'Oh my God!' whispered Flora. 'Here comes Jodie! Listen, don't mention the beach trip! Jack's parents say there's only room for two girls because they've only got one spare bedroom and that's for you and me. The boys are going to be up in the attic dorm, but girls aren't allowed up there – his parents are really strict. But let's talk about something else . . . her latest music video is amazing, isn't it?'

'I think it's a bit gross actually,' said Jess quickly. 'I so hate those pants she's wearing.'

'What pants? Who's wearing them?' demanded Jodie in her usual barging way. 'Who are we talking about?'

'I forget her name,' said Jess. 'The lead singer of the Whossnames.'

'What? The Sugababes?'

'A bit like the Sugababes, only lower calorie,' added Flora, a funny little smile rippling around her mouth. You could see she was longing to laugh. 'We've got to stop eating chocolate, Jess. Remember our resolution!'

'Got any left?' asked Jodie greedily. Mentioning

chocolate had been a stroke of genius, distracting her from the fictional singer with the awful pants. 'Remember I shared my pancake with you last Saturday.'

'Sorry,' said Jess, waving the wrapper about. 'All gone!'

'You two are so tight!' moaned Jodie.

If she was like this about the chocolate, how furious would she be if she realised she was going to miss out on Dorset?

'Oh great!' Jodie went on. 'Here comes Fred. I could do with a laugh.'

Jess and Flora exchanged a desperate glance. Fred was indeed approaching, but he didn't know that nobody was supposed to mention the beach weekend to Jodie. In seconds, they would be in even hotter water than before – it would be positively boiling.

Chapter 8

'Fred! Fred!' called Jodie unnecessarily, as Fred was coming towards them already. 'Have you worked out your stand-up routine for the dinner dance yet?'

'Not quite.' Fred went slightly pale. 'We can't agree on anything.'

Jess was annoyed that Jodie always seemed to think that Fred would be hosting the event on his own. But she couldn't afford to alienate Jodie now with a stressy jealous aside. She needed her help.

'Jodie,' she said in a friendly, coaxing voice, 'you remember you offered to help with the buffet? That was so, so nice of you.'

'What?' asked Jodie sharply. 'I never said that!'

'It was a few weeks ago,' Jess went on, smiling her most charming smile and secretly praying for divine help. 'You said you'd probably be able to help . . .'

'No, no, sorry.' Jodie backed off. 'I'm hopeless at all that stuff, and anyway, my nan is coming for the weekend – I'll have to spend all my time with her. Gotta go. See you!' She strode swiftly off towards the cloakrooms.

'Well done,' whispered Flora. 'That got rid of her.'

'Fred!' Jess grabbed his sleeve. 'We have to get going with Chaos! It's in three weeks' time!'

'I know,' said Fred. 'That's why I said going to Dorset was a bad idea, remember?'

'So what's the latest with the bands?' demanded Jess. Fred twitched in an uneasy way.

'I'm, er, negotiating with Goldilocks.'

'So nothing's fixed yet?' asked Jess fearfully. Fred shook his head. 'Oh my God!' Jess gabbled, her eyes wide, her heart pumping. 'We haven't got a band, we haven't organised any food – we've seriously got to get going with this or it'll be a disaster!'

'I was wondering, if Goldilocks aren't available, whether Poisonous Trash would like to reform, just for this one gig.' Fred turned to Flora, and the look in his eyes could only be described as desperate and pleading. Poisonous Trash was a band that Mackenzie and Ben Jones had had for a while, and Flora had been lead singer. Singing was the one thing (so far – apart from art) which Flora had been rubbish at, and the band had bombed big time.

'God, no!' Flora shuddered. 'I'd rather run naked through the town centre at Saturday lunchtime, wearing the head of a pantomime horse!'

'Hmmm.' Fred tried to look relaxed and jokey. 'Well, maybe we could work that into the cabaret, if you're offering.'

'Haven't you fixed the music up yet?' asked Flora nervously. She was kind of out of touch because she spent such a lot of time with Jack these days, and when she and Jess were together, they tended to talk incessantly about really important things like the shape of their eyebrows. 'It's getting quite near the time now, isn't it?'

'Oh, we've got a DJ,' said Jess hurriedly. 'But it's only Gordon Smith – need I say more? I mean, he's OK for short bursts, but we must have a band!'

'And what about the other stuff you were going to have?' asked Flora tactlessly. 'Fire-eaters? And lasers? And a chocolate fountain!'

Jess and Fred exchanged a panic-stricken, paralysed glance.

'Wow! Sounds like the event of the year – not counting my annual bath,' said Fred, putting on a wry smile even though Jess knew he was shuddering in fear. 'I dunno. What happened about all that stuff?'

Jess's blood froze. 'At least we haven't mentioned those things on the posters or the tickets,' she pointed out, trembling.

'Don't worry, don't worry!' said Fred. 'It'll all be all right on the night!'

'It *so* won't, unless we get our act together – and fast,' snapped Jess, exasperated.

'We'll just give it everything from now on,' said Fred. 'We can finalise everything the weekend before – have a kind of rehearsal or something.'

'But, Fred,' cried Jess in dismay, 'the weekend before is our trip to Dorset!'

'Oh, that,' muttered Fred. 'Do you really think we can manage it?' Jess felt a hot surge of anger. How could he call it 'that' in front of Flora? It was so rude! Flora and Jack had invited them for a whole weekend, and it was going to be utterly brilliant.

'Maybe you can manage both,' suggested Flora. 'You could always sort out the final details from a distance by phone or something.'

'Yeah, but . . .' Jess was feeling queasy again '. . . we'll be in Dorset – that's miles away, a hundred miles, probably!' Geography wasn't Jess's strong point. 'We'll have to have everything fixed up before we go! Oh God, this is so stressful!' Jess could feel her heart banging away against her ribs like a vicious dog trying to escape from a steel-mesh cage.

'If you get everything organised in advance,' said Flora gently, 'coming to Dorset could be a wonderful break for you both after all the hassle – you can chill out and relax before the main event. Apparently sometimes they have barbecues on the beach – that must be so cool.'

'A barbecue? In midwinter?' queried Fred.

'Fred!' Jess was seriously pissed off with his attitude. It seemed as if he was dissing Flora's house party. 'This weekend is going to be the most awesome trip ever! Winter just makes it even better! We're gonna have log fires and charades and it might even snow!' Even as she produced this advert for the Dorset weekend, however, Jess's mind was whirling. How were they going to finalise all the details for Chaos by then? How could they just drop all the organisation and take off for the beach?

Fred pulled a series of embarrassed-but-thinking faces, tossing and turning his head from side to side. 'I'm sure we can sort it all out in time,' he said. 'But you're going to have to take control. After all, as you once famously told me, *I* can't organise my way out of a paper bag! See you in English!' And he ran off along the crowded corridor.

'Fred is so goddam irresponsible,' grumbled Jess as they set off towards English. 'I have to sort all the problems out. It's always the same. This Chaos thing is going to push me right over the edge and into total insanity. We've been so stupid, letting things slide. I'm such an idiot about times and dates and stuff! I'd no idea it would clash with your lovely weekend!'

'Oh God, I hate all this!' hissed Flora. 'I wish I'd never – oh, forget it.'

'What?' Jess asked suspiciously. 'You wish what? You wish you'd never invited me and Fred?'

'No, no, no, not that! Don't be stupid! I wish it wasn't the weekend before the dinner dance, that's all.' Flora sounded rattled.

They arrived at the English lesson, where Mr Fothergill was preparing some kind of ordeal by Shakespeare. Fred was sitting with some boys at the back. Jess didn't look at him.

'Right,' said Mr Fothergill. 'You're going to enjoy this. This is the scene where an old man gets stabbed to death behind a tapestry.'

It still didn't compare to the best of the *X Files*, however, and Jess found herself walking home alone again because Fred was at a chess match against Sir John Baxter's School, a famous toffee-nosed academy in the next town. Flora, as usual, had gone off with Jack. Jess felt tragic and self-pitying, trudging the pavements on her own. Why had Fred gone off to do stupid old chess when there was such a lot of important stuff to organise? And why hadn't they organised it properly weeks ago? Why did the Dorset weekend have to be just before the dinner dance? Why had God got it in for her? She'd tried her hardest to avoid chocolate.

'Good news,' said Granny, as Jess entered the kitchen. 'I've just made a chocolate cake, and it's a belter.'

'I was supposed to not eat so much chocolate, Granny,' Jess reminded her. 'I made a new year's resolution not to eat chocolate more than twice a month because of my spots and my massive flabby hips.'

'Oh, don't worry about that, love,' Granny assured her. 'You're the prettiest girl in the street.'

'The street?' complained Jess. 'That's a bit small-scale. How about the country, the world, the universe?

That's more the kind of reassurance I'm looking for.'

'Oh, the universe, then,' said Granny. 'I hear those girls from Outer Space are all warts and tentacles, though, so it's hardly much competition.'

Jess threw her school bag in the corner and got a smoothie out of the fridge. 'Any good murders today?' she enquired politely, though her mind was still miserably obsessed with the Chaos chaos.

'Not really,' said Granny. 'Although I did watch a Miss Marple this afternoon. *The Body in the Library*. One of my favourites. Set by the sea down in Devon.'

'Oh, Granny.' Jess felt an overpowering urge to share her angst with somebody who wouldn't be too judgemental. 'I've done something stupid – that weekend in Dorset is just before our dinner dance and we haven't really started organising it properly yet.'

'Not started organising it yet?' Granny looked amused. 'Tell me all about it, dear!'

Chapter 9

Somehow Jess had hoped Granny would come up with some kind of magic solution, but all she said, after shaking her head and tut-tutting a bit, was, 'Let me think about it, sweetheart.'

Jess knew that Granny would forget all about her Chaos crisis if there was a particularly gruesome murder on the news. She'd probably forget all about it anyway. Granny was getting a bit forgetful these days. She'd called Jess Madeleine last week – that was Mum's name.

'Please, God,' murmured Jess as she climbed the stairs, 'don't let Granny get dementia. And if you could possibly organise Chaos for us, that would obviously be a bonus.' Poor God was going to have his work cut out, but when it came to organising Chaos, he'd be your obvious first choice.

Jess checked her emails and found the latest instalment of *Lord of the Wrongs* from Dad.

. . . Lord Volcano stared, baffled, at the magic shoes. He'd plugged them in and charged them overnight, but he still didn't have the faintest idea what kind of magic shoes they were; the instructions were in Fishish, and where was he going to find a fish to translate for him? He gazed longingly at the sea below. It must be full of fish. And then a strange thought occurred to him. Why were the instructions in Fishish anyway? Fish don't have feet, do they? Hmmm. There was something fishy going on here . . .

Maybe these magic shoes weren't really a present from his long-lost daughter Messica after all. Maybe it was a secret trap, a cruel trick being played on him by Sir Filo Pastry. Maybe they were truth shoes, and the moment he put them on, he'd blurt out all his secrets. Sir Filo Pastry, he knew, would be watching his every move on CCTV. Sir F would be waiting for him to reveal the location of his magnificent treasure, the shimmering Pot of Gold.

If they were the kind of magic shoes that enable you to jump confidently off window sills and soar effortlessly into the clouds, he'd be able to escape right now. On the other hand, they might be the kind of magic shoes that would turn you into a silver teapot. And handsome though silver teapots can be, Lord Volcano didn't really fancy having boiling water poured in through a hole in his head on a regular basis. It wasn't what he would have called a lifestyle.

Thoughtfully he plucked his familiar, Donald, out of his cosy thatched matchbox.

'Donald,' he said, 'I have a task for you. Go to my long-lost daughter who lives two hundred miles away through the forests of Pog, and ask her if indeed she really did send me these magic shoes and, if so, how on earth you're supposed to switch them on.'

'But, Master,' said Donald with a puzzled frown, 'I'm a blinking snail! It'll take me three weeks just to get down the wall of this blinking tower!'

Jess paused in thought. It was a relief to think about something other than a dinner dance. She started to type.

'I've thought of that, of course,' said Lord Volcano with a sneer. Sometimes he wished his familiar was something intelligent and stylish, like a dolphin, but his bath, though large, really wasn't big enough for an ocean-going mammal. 'Donald, you're an idiot. I've made a little motor for you — it's a bit like a racing-car engine but, obviously, scaled down.'

With a few deft movements of his long webbed fingers, Lord Volcano attached the motor to the back of Donald's shell and pressed the electronic ignition. It roared into life – in a tiny, tinkling way, a bit like a wasp in a jam jar – and propelled Donald violently across the window sill and down the wall of the tower.

'Help!' cried Donald faintly, and, to be honest, slimily. 'I don't even know where she lives!'

'Don't worry!' called Lord Volcano. 'You've got SnailNav! Just switch it on!'

'But how?' screamed Donald in alarm, as he reached ground level and scorched away through the grass like a dropped firework. Before Lord Volcano could utter a word, poor Donald had vanished.

If only there really was such a thing as magic, thought Jess, sending the email and staring blankly into space. If only she could order a dinner dance to be delivered to St Mark's Church Hall on 14th February at 7.30 p.m. And it would help if she could see right into the mind of Fred. Knowing what he was thinking was sometimes so tricky. The witty banter they shared was the best thing in her life, but witty banter wasn't always appropriate. Sometimes there was serious stuff to talk about, problems to wrestle with. Where was Fred then? In fact, where was Fred now?

She picked up her mobile and hesitated. Should she call him? They had to organise the buffet and the band, if nothing else. Maybe she should ring Dad and ask his advice. Although, strangely, since they'd started writing this book together, they hadn't communicated by text or phone as they normally did.

She dialled Dad's landline (he was always losing his mobile). It rang twice and then somebody picked up.

'Hi, Phil speaking.'

'Oh, hi, Phil. This is Jess. How are you?' Phil, Dad's boyfriend, was great and really, really funny.

'Oh, good thanks, Jess. How about you?'

'Oh, fine. Just the usual crises and fiascos.'

'Life, huh?'

'Yeah. Er, is Dad there?'

'No, sorry, Jess. He's out. Can I give him a message?'

'No, it's OK – just say I rang. If he rings back remind him not to use the landline after ten or Mum goes ballistic.'

'Will do!' Phil laughed. There was a slight pause. 'Sorry, Jess, but I've got to go now, I'm in the middle of something. Give my best to your mum.'

'OK. Lots of love! Bye!'

'Bye!' He hung up.

Jess listened to the purr of the dead telephone line. It was a shame Phil had been too busy to talk properly. He'd sounded a little bit preoccupied. Maybe Dad had left a pile of dirty dishes in the sink or something.

Later that evening, after Granny had gone out to see her friend Deborah, Mum got out her laptop.

'I'm going to give it one more go,' she said, looking serious.

'What?' Jess was beginning to wonder if one last tiny slice of chocolate cake would hurt. She'd only had three very small ones, and she didn't want Granny to think she was ungrateful.

'This online dating thing,' said Mum. 'I don't think I should give up too easily, just because Ken was a bit smelly. There's a guy here who might be quite interesting. He actually does look a bit like Mel Gibson – one of my favourite hunks.'

'Let me see!' Jess bounded over and stared at the screen. 'Hmmm . . . Mel Gibson after a nose transplant, maybe.'

'He's divorced with a teenage daughter,' Mum

went on. 'That's partly what attracted me to him.'

'Don't drag me into it!' Jess backed off.

'I thought maybe you could be friends . . . ?'

'I've already got friends! Mum, I'm not being mean, but you should be thinking about what you want, not about me.'

'Well, he does look rather nice. His name's Ed and he's a builder.'

'A builder?' Jess was surprised. Somehow she'd expected him to have one of those arty jobs.

'I thought maybe he could help me with the built-in storage project for my office,' said Mum.

'Mum! This is a dating website, right? If you want him to fix your cupboards and stuff, that's something totally different.'

'Hmmm, I suppose so,' said Mum doubtfully. She really wasn't focusing properly on this dating business. 'I thought maybe we could all go out together as a foursome – you know, me and you and him and, er, Polly. His daughter's called Polly.'

'Not Polymyalgia Rheumatica? Are you sure she's not an awful disease? Honestly, Mum, you don't really want your date to be a foursome?'

'You know, it's always a bit easier if there are more than just two of you.'

'But, Mum, *you're* the one who's supposed to be dating this guy.'

'Well, if you like him and we all get on, maybe he and I could go out on our own at a later stage. I thought it would be nice, first, if we could all go to a movie and have a pizza afterwards.'

'This is weird.'

'Oh, please, Jess! You were so helpful when I needed to get rid of Ken. It's a bit strange dating after all these years. It's fourteen years since Dad and I split up.'

'Fine.' Jess shrugged awkwardly. 'Fix it up. I'll be there. Not the weekend after next, though – I'll be in Dorset. I assume I'm allowed to go?' Actually, agreeing to the foursome with Ed the Builder and Polly the Daughter was a useful bargaining tool for getting Mum on side about the Dorset trip, even though, secretly, Jess was beginning to think of the weekend at the beach as a huge obstacle to organising the dinner dance. This was such a shame – normally a trip to the sea with her best friends would have been the high point of her year.

'All right, but I reserve the right to reorganise your travel plans if there's any more talk of Jack driving you down.'

Jess sighed heavily. Mum's phobias really made life hard sometimes. 'OK, OK,' she agreed. 'Now I've got to go upstairs and answer a few emails.'

'You have done your homework, haven't you?' asked Mum suspiciously.

'Of course!' lied Jess with a smile. Poor Mum! Little did she know that not only had Jess not done her homework yet, but that she had forged Mum's signature in the homework book to confirm that she *had* done it. Mum didn't even know the homework book existed. Jess had forged Mum's signature every day since the start of the school year back in September. In fact, forging Mum's signature was the nearest Jess had come to satisfying creative work recently – apart from designing the Chaos tickets.

Later on, Jess conjured up her inbox. Nothing from Dad. He hadn't rung, either, and he probably wouldn't now, because it was after ten and talking on mobiles was expensive – and he knew that Mum didn't like him calling Jess on her mobile for long chats because Mum was convinced that mobiles were bad for you. He could have sent an email, though. Jess wasn't sure Dad would have any useful input about the dinner dance anyway. And she still didn't want to tell Mum, because she knew Mum would go ballistic.

An email from Fred suddenly popped into view. Eagerly, Jess opened it.

Maybe we should do some more work on our routine for Chaos? I've gone off meerkats. Any ideas?

Any ideas? Any ideas? Jess seethed with rage. Didn't Fred understand that they had many more important things to fix than their routine? How can you have a dinner dance without dinner or dancing? Jess was too furious to reply.

Chapter 10

Just as she was taking off her make-up, Jess realised that her dad hadn't rung back. This was annoying. Usually, when she phoned Dad and Phil answered, they'd have a good old chat and then he'd get Dad to return her call the minute he came home. Jess grabbed her mobile and called Dad on his mobile. It was worth killing a few brain cells just to make sure nothing was wrong with the old boy.

'Hi, Messica!' He sounded just fine.

'Dad! Or should I say, Lord Volcano?'

'How are you, old bean?'

'Good! But why didn't you call me back? I rang earlier and left a message with Phil.'

'Oh, yes, sorry, I forgot. I've got so much on my mind at the moment – if you can call it a mind.'

'How's lovely St Ives?' Jess could easily picture his

fabulous house with the sea sparkling nearby and the gulls screaming overhead. 'And how's Phil? He didn't have time to talk. He said he was busy.'

'Oh, he's cooking up this new project – uh – he's thinking of starting up a new boutique in Barcelona.'

'Barcelona?'

'Yup. Erm, yes.'

'Where is Barcelona again?' Though Jess's geography was appalling, she had a feeling it wasn't the next village along from St Ives.

'Spain, last time I looked.'

'Oh, amazing! You'll be able to have lots of lovely trips there! Is it by the sea?'

'Yes, and it's a wonderful city.' Dad sounded wistful, as if he was longing to go there right now. 'It's got a very special cathedral.'

'Never mind the cathedral! Lead me to those beaches! I will be able to come and see you, won't I? Will you be moving there completely or will Phil just be going to and from Cornwall?'

'I don't really know. It's all up in the air at the moment. He's trying to raise some capital. He needs backers.'

'Well, tell him he can have next week's pocket money!' Jess felt so excited about Phil's new project.

'As long as I can have a weekend in Barcelona some-time.'

'Of course you can.'

At this point Mum knocked on Jess's door. 'Jess!' she called. 'Are you talking on your mobile? You know I don't like you doing that. Your mobile is for emergencies!'

'It's only Dad!' yelled Jess. Mum opened the door and peeked in.

'Did he ring? Honestly! He knows my views on mobiles!'

'No, no, I rang him,' insisted Jess.

'I'd better go,' said Dad. 'I can hear trouble brewing.'

Oh no! She hadn't had time to ask Dad's advice about organising the dinner dance, and now she couldn't mention it with Mum standing there. Disaster! She had killed thousands of brain cells for nothing!

Once the call ended, Mum looked relieved that the brain-radiation danger was past. Instead of giving Jess a hard time about it (certainly one of her usual options), she sat down gingerly on the bed and waggled her feet about. This was always a sign that she had something slightly dodgy to say.

77

'It's all arranged,' she said.

'What is?' Jess felt a spear of fear. Her mum arranging things was often bad news, involving dentists and trips to museums.

'The outing with Ed the Builder and his daughter Molly – er, Polly.'

Jess's heart sank. Still, she had to endure this in order to keep Mum sweet about the weekend in Dorset. Although maybe it would be a good thing if Mum said she couldn't go to Dorset after all – then she would be forced to stay at home and concentrate on Chaos. Life was so confusing at the moment.

'We're going to the new James Bond film and then we're going to have pizza afterwards,' said Mum doubtfully.

'Sounds perfect!' Jess beamed. It seemed Mum needed a bit of reassurance. 'It'll be great!'

Once Mum had gone away, Jess lay down in bed, but she didn't switch off her bedside light. She stared at the ceiling, haunted by the awful thought that there was so little time before Chaos. She'd been thrilled when their poster campaign, plus a lot of word-of-mouth boasting, had resulted in huge interest and the tickets had been snapped up like hot cakes. Yes, ninety-two people were going to be turning up at St Mark's Church Hall on 14th February, all kitted out in their best and expecting a good time. And they'd paid for it. Jess so desperately wanted to put on a good show for them, but organising the details was almost driving her round the bend.

Suddenly Jess remembered the envelope bursting with cheques and cash – she must count it, and tomorrow after school she and Fred could go into the bank, open an account and stash the money safely away. She threw open the wardrobe doors, and peered into the gloom. There was a tumbled heap of clothes in the bottom of the wardrobe, as usual. Jess knelt down and tossed the clothes aside. There were her best party shoes – black patent leather, with wicked heels. Her toes twinged at the sight of them. And there was her second-best pair of trainers, which she thought she'd lost! But where was the plastic box?

Jess's heart gave a sickening lurch. She grabbed all the remaining items of clothing and hurled them backwards over her head, until the bottom of the wardrobe was quite clear, apart from shoes. The box was gone! For a mad, blind moment she thought somebody must have nicked it. Could somebody have tricked their way in here, telling Granny they were from the government's Wardrobe Inspection Scheme?

Granny hadn't said anything about it.

For an even madder moment Jess wondered if Granny – or even Mum – had stolen the box themselves. No, no, that was insane. But where was it? Heart thumping in anguish, Jess sat back on her heels, closed her eyes and tried to remember the day she'd stashed the cheques away. All she could remember was getting into a bit of an anxious spin back then, and trying several different hiding places. She leapt to her feet and pulled out the drawers of her dressing table.

She was faced with half a bar of very old chocolate, a button off her new jacket, a ballpoint pen showing a muscle man (whose pants descended when the pen was tipped up), a teaspoon, a library membership card with tea stains on it, a miniature elephant wearing a tutu (in plastic), a key ring shaped like a sports car . . . so many treasures, but not the slightest trace of any cheques or cash.

Socks! Jess remembered stuffing some notes into a sock! She pulled out her sock drawer and thrust her hand into sock after sock. Wait! A crackle! Banknotes! £75, the price of a double ticket. But whose was it? Jess's blood ran cold. Why hadn't she kept better records?

Suddenly Mum burst in without knocking. She

looked puzzled and a bit fraught.

'Jess, turn your light off! It's eleven o'clock! You've got school tomorrow!' Then she took in the mess. 'What on earth have you been doing?' She gazed around, horrified.

'Just looking for something,' said Jess, scrunching the banknotes up in her hand. She felt so guilty – but why? She was organising this thing perfectly legitimately – the money in her hand was somebody's payment, which she was perfectly entitled to have. It was the utter chaos of her performance so far that filled her with guilt. She couldn't bear Mum to know how crap she had been at organising this. Mum would have a fit.

'Looking for what?' demanded Mum.

'Uh, m-my old purse,' stammered Jess in a flap. 'It had . . . my History Club card in it.'

'History Club?' Mum seemed strangely, inconveniently charmed by this idea. 'I didn't know there was a History Club.' No wonder she didn't know – Jess had only just invented it.

'Yes.' Jess stood up and started throwing socks back into the drawer. 'It's boring, really.'

'History's not boring!' cried Mum in rapture. 'What do you do?'

'Oh, we have meetings and talks about historical people, you know.' Jess tried to sound bored. 'Sometimes there are trips to . . . old buildings and stuff.'

'What old buildings?'

'Oh, you know, churches and things . . .'

'Which churches have you been to?' asked Mum, clearly thrilled.

'None.' Jess hated to disappoint her, but she had to draw a veil over this fictional club ASAP. 'I didn't go because basically I hate churches – no offence, God.'

'Of course you don't hate churches!' cried Mum in dismay. 'Remember St Petrock's in Parracombe?'

Jess gave her a blank stare. 'Sorry, no.'

'That lovely little church we saw on our way back from visiting Dad in St Ives!' Mum raved on. 'You said it was the loveliest church you'd ever seen!' Jess remembered, now, how saying that had been part of a bigger plan to deserve an ice cream once they arrived in a proper town.

'Mum, I'll tell you more about History Club tomorrow, OK? And I'll tidy my room in the morning.' Jess lay down in bed, yawned and tried to look sleepy, though she had never felt less dozy – the thought that she had managed to lose thousands of pounds had set off a kind of electrical storm in her tummy.

'OK, then,' Mum said, and kissed her on the cheek. 'Sleep well, love!'

Jess lay down and closed her eyes as Mum switched off the light and went out. Instantly Jess's eyes snapped open and she grabbed her phone. Under the covers she started texting away like mad.

HAVE YOU GOT CHEQUES OR CASH FOR CHAOS? MAJOR PANIC: CAN'T FIND ANY HERE!

Five minutes later a reply arrived from Fred: **NO, THINK YOU HAD THE MUNS. REMEMBER YOU WOULDN'T TRUST ME WIV IT? HA HA! HAVE LOOKED EVERYWHERE, EVEN IN MY RIGHT NOSTRIL (USUAL HIDING PLACE FOR TOP-SECRET ITEMS) BUT NO LUCK. CU TOMORROW X**

God! How could Fred joke at a time like this? Jess threw her phone violently across the room. It landed softly, somewhere on a pile of clothes. If it rang in the night she wouldn't be able to find it in the dark and it might wake Mum up and she'd be hopping mad. Jess clenched her eyes tightly shut. When was this nightmare going to end? What had she done with the money?

Chapter 11

At school next day Jess and Fred argued, privately (at the edge of the football pitch to avoid being over-heard), about who had last had the bundle of cheques and cash.

'Look, it's bound to be somewhere,' Fred tried to reassure her. 'It'll be in your bedroom, right?'

'Or your bedroom!' Jess insisted. 'Listen, Fred, you've got to go home this evening and ransack your room! In fact, I'll come and help!'

'Ransack your own room!' retorted Fred. 'You're not coming snooping about in mine! I have weapons of mass destruction stashed away in there! Anyway, I'm busy after school today – there's Chess Club practice.'

'Fred, you *have* to help me organise this dinner dance! Put Chess Club on hold for a few days!'

'Sorry.' Fred started walking backwards, away from her; one of his infuriating habits when cornered. 'No need to panic for another forty-eight hours, though, is there?' He raised an eyebrow in a way that Jess occasionally found lovable. But not now. A full-scale panic had already got going in her insides; her tum had dissolved into a kind of bubbling witch's cauldron.

That evening Jack had a rugby match and Fred had his precious Chess Club, so it was a chance for Jess and Flora to walk home together. Jess hadn't mentioned the money crisis to Flora, because, of course, it was Flora's family's money as well as everybody else's that she had lost. Instead she tried to enter into a slightly feverishly festive mood.

'God, it feels like a treat to have some time to ourselves!' sighed Jess. 'Men! Aren't they just a waste of space!'

'Totally,' agreed Flora with her rippling laugh. 'Oh my God, it's so cold! Where's my hat?' She pulled her fur-trapper's hat out of her school bag and rammed it on her head. Flora didn't usually wear hats, because she thought they made her hair go limp and horrid, but today was so cold, the pavements seemed to be made of iron.

'God, totally arctic,' agreed Jess, snuggling into her scarf. It was already getting dark – they'd stopped for a hot choc at the Dolphin Cafe – and now their breath billowed in the faint glow of the street lamps.

'What time is it?' Flora looked at her watch for the hundredth time that day.

'Stop showing off that goddam watch.' Jess grinned. 'I know your boyfriend is a billionaire and never stops loading you with bling, but we Neanderthals do have feelings, you know. My only watch came out of a cracker.'

'Shut up! Don't be an idiot!' Flora laughed, admiring the watch again before plunging her hand back into her sheepskin mitt. 'It was rather fabulous of him, though.'

'I can't imagine what it's like having a boyfriend who spends over a hundred pounds on you!' Jess shook her head. 'I'm trying to imagine Fred spending anything on me at all. He's notoriously tight.' It seemed impossible to get away from the horrible subject of money. 'Fred did write me a poem once, but he even asked me for the paper to write it on.'

'Oh, but Jack could never write a poem!' cried Flora. 'You're the lucky one! Fred is so clever! Jack is, like, totally without imagination.'

'All the same – that watch . . .'

'He did get it cheap off the internet, and it was a sort of late Christmas present. And he did earn quite a lot working on his dad's business website.'

'OK, OK,' smiled Jess. 'I'm just dead jealous of you, you pampered bitch!'

Flora laughed, and a cute little twinkly pair of dimples appeared on the flawless jewel of her face.

Once home, Jess turned her room upside down. There was still no sign of the money. She racked her brains. In the early stages when people had been buying tickets, she and Fred had tossed the envelope of money to and fro like a hot potato, always meaning to open a bank account for it and never getting round to it, making a kind of joke – a joke! – about who was more likely to lose it. But her bedroom was totally and utterly ransacked – she had flung all her possessions about in a kind of panicky madness – and there just wasn't any money anywhere. That was a fact.

Fred must have it – even though he'd texted her to say he didn't, she secretly suspected that he hadn't even started to look yet, because he was sure that she had it. But of course she *didn't* have it, so he must have it, and as soon as Fred started to look in the enormous pile of debris that formed his approach to interior design, he would certainly find it. This reassured her slightly, and she was able, at last, to think of other things, some of them potentially just as awful, but in new, exciting ways.

On Saturday night Jess had to prepare for the ludicrous double date with Mum, Ed the Builder and Polly. He already sounded like a character on a children's TV programme. Jess was half expecting him to be constructed of cheerful yellow plastic, with a detachable head. As for his daughter Polly, it was essential that Jess manage to look cooler than her. Although not knowing what Polly was like was a slight disadvantage when planning what to wear.

At first she let rip, in the privacy of her bedroom, with a pink sequinned vest, cute black jacket and black drainpipe jeans. Were her legs thin enough for drainpipes, though? What if Polly was also wearing drainpipes, only her legs were endless and slim? Jess went downstairs and confronted Granny, who was watching a documentary about Jack the Ripper.

'Granny! Look! Do I look OK?'

'Lovely, dear,' Granny assured her, dragging her eyes with reluctance from a period homicide. Then she focussed. 'Is it a disco you're going to?'

'No, Granny! It's that double date with Bob the Builder – sorry, Ed – and his stupid daughter.'

'Don't you like her, then?' asked Granny.

'Well, I haven't actually met her yet,' said Jess irritably, 'but I expect she'll turn out to be Miss Totally Goddam Perfect.'

Granny looked thoughtfully at her ensemble. 'What is it again – pizza?'

'Yes, a movie then pizza.'

'Well, dear, don't be upset . . .'

'Of course I won't be upset! I need your advice.'

'Well, I do think you might have overdone it a bit.'

Jess was upset.

'You look a bit – how shall I put it? – like a Christmas tree decoration.'

Jess was outraged. 'Granny, how dare you!' she yelled, managing – just – to keep it good-natured. 'I wanted your input, not a character assassination.'

'Well, you can never go wrong if you're *under*-dressed, dear,' explained Granny, her eyes swerving towards the irresistible TV screen. 'In the sixties, we all wore sequins all day: girls, boys, dogs, the lot. But nowadays it does look a bit – dressy.'

Jess ran back upstairs, threw off her sparkles and

89

pulled on jeans and a stretchy leopard-print top. A Christmas tree decoration? Honestly!

They'd agreed to meet in a little cafe called Gino's, near the cinema. Mum was holding on so tightly to Jess's arm, they were both getting pins and needles in their hands.

'I tried on about thirty outfits this evening,' whispered Mum as they approached Gino's – quite slowly, as Mum had got her high heels out of mothballs and was teetering along the pavement in a rather worrying way, as if a trip and a sprawl weren't entirely off the cards.

'You look great,' Jess told her. Mum was wearing her dark dress, the one she always used for winter funerals, with a little grey and pink cardy to soften it up. It was all, however, hidden by her massive quilted coat, which made her look like a walking duvet – though Jess didn't have the heart to say so. She left that kind of hurtful truth-telling to her tactless grandmother.

'Why ever did I let myself in for this?' groaned Mum as they reached the door of Gino's.

'Never mind you!' growled Jess. 'Why did you let *me* in for it? How are we going to recognise them?'

'He said he'd be wearing a denim jacket,' said

Mum, 'and he promised we'd notice Polly as soon as we got inside.'

'What's so goddam special about this precious Polly?' grumbled Jess. Then they barged into the cafe and saw her.

Chapter 12

Polly was a goth. Her face was chalky white, her hair was a dyed-red Mohican, she was wearing a kind of black fishnet top under a black leather jacket, and she had so many piercings that when she turned her head towards them, her face tinkled.

'Wow!' muttered Jess. 'We're into hardcore gothic here.'

'Shush!' hissed Mum. 'Come on!' Barging clumsily between the cafe tables in her duvet coat, she headed for the person she guessed must be Ed the Builder, a man with a gut so massive you would've thought he was expecting twins. He had close-cropped ginger hair and his face was covered with freckles. The faint resemblance to Mel Gibson which Mum had noticed in his photo was mysteriously absent in person.

'Ed?' Mum said, sweeping a fork off a nearby table

with her air bag arm. 'I'm Madeleine. And this is Jess.'

Ed made a clumsy half-hearted attempt to get to his feet, but he struck the cafe table with his paunch and sat down heavily again.

'Don't get up! Don't get up!' cried Mum. 'This place is so crowded! Hello, you must be Polly.'

Polly looked challengingly at them and raised an eyebrow that was already kind of savage and sharpened. 'Hiya,' she said. Her voice was sweet and low and actually quite friendly.

'Cool jacket,' said Jess with as genuine a smile as possible in the rather weird circumstances. Polly smiled, and she instantly looked much less scary.

'Yeah, I got it in this awesome ex-government surplus place in, like, London. My boyfriend Wills knows one of the guys who works there – he's, like, his cousin's friend and he's got these amazing tattoos of, like, lions and stuff.'

Ed turned his head and gave his daughter a rather hard look. Polly glared defiantly at him.

'What?' she demanded. 'What!?' He turned back to Mum and shrugged.

'She's after tattoos,' he said. These were the first words he had addressed to Mum. Jess was fairly sure it wasn't the recommended greeting in the *How to Woo Fair Ladies and Sweep Them off Their Feet Handbook*.

'So what if I am!' hissed Polly at her dad. 'It's my body, isn't it?'

'You know what I think,' he informed her crisply. Then, disastrously, he turned to Mum. 'What's your view, Madeleine?' he enquired, leaning back in his chair and tapping his paunch thoughtfully. 'Would you let Jessica have tattoos?'

'Don't drag me into it!' laughed Mum, but in a way that was about as far from amusement as it's possible to be. 'Jess hasn't made any plans for tattoos yet, and I'm not sure how I'd react.'

Jess was imagining, in the way that one's mind plays tricks, how Ed would look if a map of the world was tattooed on his belly. It could lead to a variation on that old song, *He's Got the Whole World on His Paunch*. He could go round the schools and be used as a visual aid in geography lessons, like a globe.

'You wouldn't want tattoos, would you now, Jessica?' demanded Ed.

Jess stared at his freckly face. 'I'm not sure.' She didn't want to side with him or his daughter. As they were doomed to spend the rest of the evening together, she decided she would pass the time by imagining what fun it would be to approach his freckly face with a felt-tip pen in a jolly join-the-dots sort of mood. She thought she could see a potential church right there on his left cheek – or was it a unicorn?

'I must get out of this coat, Jess.' Mum turned to her for help. The chairs were small and somehow nastily curved, so once seated in them you could easily start to feel as if you'd never get out, especially if you were swaddled up in five kilos of polyester wadding. 'Help me, love!' appealed Mum.

Jess caught her eye for a split second, and they shared a deeper moment of understanding than they had ever experienced before. Mum was wishing her daughter had been born with supernatural powers and was able not just to help her out of her duvet coat, but to sweep her up under her arm and fly off, smashing the cafe window to smithereens as they passed, rocket-like, through it and headed for Zanzibar.

Jess was wondering why she had been born to this ridiculous woman caught up in her disastrous dating madness, when, if there was any justice, her mum could have been Sharon Osbourne or Meryl Streep.

However, she just gritted her teeth and pulled the duvet coat off, then sat down and shared with Polly a kind of eyebrows-raised *Isn't my parent appalling?* shrug, which was the nearest they were going to get to bonding.

The film was OK, because they just sat in a row in the darkness (why couldn't all relationships be like that?). But chatting in the pizzeria afterwards was always going to be a challenge . . .

'So, Polly,' said Mum, reaching deep into her emergency store of librarian's conversational gambits, 'have you read any good books recently?'

Polly looked startled. At this point, mercifully perhaps, Jess's phone bleeped. She scrabbled in her bag.

'You should turn that thing off when we're having dinner,' said Mum irritably.

'Oh, don't mind us!' Ed waved Jess on as if Mum's etiquette was absurd. 'Pol's texting away day and night.'

'Only my mum!' Polly said, shooting her dad a secret fierce look. 'I text my mum, right, because I hardly ever see her.'

'All right, all right, don't let's go through all that again!' Ed flapped his arms at his daughter. It was a strange gesture, like trying to scare birds off a picnic table.

Jess took a peek at her phone. **MESSICA! LATEST EPISODE IS FESTERING IN YOUR INBOX. DREADFUL DISASTERS BESET LORD VOLCANO.**

'Who's it from?' asked Mum. 'Fred?'

'No, Dad.' Jess swiftly composed a reply suggesting that whatever disasters had befallen Lord Volcano they couldn't compete with her own current night out from hell.

'So, you been divorced long, Madeleine?' enquired Ed, picking his teeth languorously in a manner designed to increase his sex appeal.

'Oh, yes, for years.' Mum brushed a few crumbs off the table and tipped them back on to her plate. 'We separated soon after Jess was born.'

'So you ruined your parents' marriage, eh, Jessica?' enquired Ed with a rather horrid and tactless grin, as if joking about such matters was just the thing to make the evening go with a swing. Jess herself had made that joke a hundred times, but coming from Ed it seemed cheeky and presumptuous.

'No, I didn't ruin it,' she explained. 'They managed that all by themselves. Dad's gay.'

There was a sudden strange silence. A weird

embarrassed expression came over Ed's face.

'Ah,' he said, rubbing his nose (always a negative gesture). 'Different!'

'Yes,' admitted Mum uneasily. 'He certainly is different.'

'He did you no good at all, then, Madeleine?' remarked Ed, staring at Mum with a mixture of disbelief and pity. 'Not very easy for you, neither, Jessica, having a Dad who's a little bit queer.'

'Oh no!' Jess felt furious. 'Everybody at school's jealous. They all think it's amazingly cool.'

'I told you so, Dad!' snapped Polly. 'You shouldn't be so homophobic.'

'Homophobic be damned,' said Ed crossly, folding his arms defensively over his enormous gut. 'I'm just a normal bloke.'

Much later that night, when they had escaped at last and were having a late-night cup of hot choc, Mum announced that her dating experiment was at an end, and that from now on she would do anything to avoid spending another evening, or even five minutes, in the company of a 'normal bloke'. Jess wondered if Mum was being a little harsh. Polly and Jess had exchanged phone numbers and email addresses – she wouldn't mind seeing Polly again some time, even if their parents' first date was going to be their last.

When Jess finally gained the sanctuary of her own room and checked her emails, the latest episode from Lord Volcano was waiting.

'I know you, Volcano,' hissed Sir Filo Pastry from the depths of his cloud-blue cloak. 'I know you're plotting against me. We intercepted your snail.'

'Not Donald!' cried Lord Volcano in alarm.

'We're debriefing him now.' Sir Filo Pastry nodded menacingly. 'He's singing like a canary.'

Lord Volcano uttered a strangled cry. Please, don't let them torture poor Donald! *he prayed.*

'And when we've got every bit of info out of him, we're going to have him boiled with garlic butter and a fine Chianti,' concluded Sir Filo Pastry. 'But as for you, Volcano,' continued the evil Sir F, 'you're going to be taken out to sea and set adrift in a small boat with only enough peanut butter sandwiches to last until Sunday.' And with a diabolical echoing laugh, he was gone. The door slammed.

Lord Volcano shuddered. Would he ever see his beloved long-lost daughter Messica again?

Chapter 13

On Sunday at lunchtime the gang met in the Dolphin Cafe. The old Dolphin was looking good: the walls had been repainted a Caribbean turquoise for the new year, and there were new twirling mobiles of dolphins, made of beautiful twinkling silver and glass. But Maria, the cafe owner, looked more melancholy than ever. She had a tendency towards heartbreak; in fact, she'd already had three heartbreaks since Christmas.

Jess, Fred, Flora, Ben Jones, Mackenzie, Jodie and Tiffany bagged the biggest table and ordered some drinks. But for once Jess didn't feel hungry: that morning, she and Fred had exchanged tense and stressy text messages about the missing money. Fred insisted that he'd searched his bedroom from top to bottom and hadn't found it; Jess was equally sure he hadn't even looked. They couldn't mention it in front of everybody, though: it was the elephant in the room.

'Have you written your stand-up for Chaos yet?' Jodie asked Fred.

He shook his head and looked embarrassed. 'No, no, I was busy all week embroidering lampshades,' said Fred. It was a kind of lame gag by his standards, but everybody laughed. Normally Jess loved the way everybody laughed at Fred's jokes, but she was in such a peculiar mood today, she didn't seem able to cope with it. Instead she felt a sudden urge to lay it all on the line (except for the missing money, of course) and fess up to the mess.

'Listen, guys,' she said. 'Fred and I are a bit out of our depth organising this Chaos thing. We could use some help.'

'Leave it with me,' said Mackenzie. 'I think it needs a Wild West motif.'

'Shut it, Mackenzie, you prat,' murmured Ben, giving Jess a quick, worried glance. Mackenzie, being Ben's best buddy, subsided slightly.

'What help do you need?' asked Jodie.

'Uh . . . quite a bit,' admitted Jess, glancing at Fred. He was stroking the edge of the table, as if distancing himself from the mess, and avoiding looking at her. Great. Fantastic. She had become invisible, less interesting than furniture. One day soon Fred might announce his engagement to a chest of drawers. 'We, er, haven't managed to get a band, for a start,' Jess went on. 'Have we, Fred? Are you still negotiating with Goldilocks?'

'Not really,' Fred admitted shiftily. 'They let me down, to be honest.'

'So, still no band,' said Jess grimly. 'Fred's dad is running the bar, because he did that heaps of times when he was in the army, but the food . . . well, I don't know where to start.'

'Pizza?' suggested Jodie, whose greed was famous throughout the south of England.

'You can't have pizza at a dinner dance!' objected Flora. 'We've got to have a proper buffet with cold chicken and stuff.'

'What's the, uh, budget?' asked Ben Jones.

Jess's heart gave a nervous leap. A budget! Of course! They should have had a budget. Her mouth went dry with panic.

'I – I'm not sure . . .' she faltered.

'Oh, Jess, you retard!' sneered Jodie. 'Don't say you don't even know what your budget is?' She glanced swiftly at Ben Jones, as if she belonged to his club of people who were savvy enough to understand the concept of budgets.

'It doesn't matter,' said Ben. 'The tickets were, uh, seventy-five pounds per couple, right?'

'So that's thirty-seven pounds fifty per person,' added Flora, the Queen of Maths.

'How much of that is going to pay for the food?' asked Tiffany, biting her nails in a lazy yet charismatic manner. Jess was jealous of her for a moment. To Tiffany, this whole conversation was just something to pass the time on a gloomy Sunday. She didn't have to organise it. Tiffany hadn't organised a party since the awful occasion of the minestrone-soup bra inserts – Jess shuddered at the memory. But if there were embarrassing moments in Jess's past, that was nothing compared to the terrible looming crisis: in less than a fortnight, Chaos would be breaking over her head like a thunderstorm.

'I don't know! I don't know!' Jess was panicking now.

'Thirty-seven quid?' Mackenzie shook his head. 'Get real! You guys have massively undercharged. This is a dinner dance, right? I saw tickets for a dinner dance in Monterey advertised on the internet for five hundred dollars!'

'You're right, the sky's the limit,' murmured Fred ironically. 'Why stop at five hundred? Why not make it an even nine? We can always ask for an extra eight hundred pounds per person on the door.'

All this jokey talk of money when they had lost thousands of pounds made Jess feel desperate and faint.

'What other expenses are there apart from food?' asked Ben Jones, rubbing his beautiful right hand across the gorgeous blond stubble of his head. 'Sorry if I'm being stupid . . .'

'Hire of the hall, for a start,' said Jodie. 'How much was that?' She turned unexpectedly to Flora.

'Me?' Flora looked startled. 'How should I know? How much was it, Jess?' It seemed Flora wanted to distance herself, too. Well, that was only fair: ultimately it was Jess and Fred who had cooked up this almighty mess, all by themselves.

'I don't remember!' Jess felt as if she was being tied up with sticky tape, like an insect struggling in a spider's web. 'Fred's dad booked the hall for us at the same time as getting the bar licence. How much was it all, Fred?'

Fred looked clueless and gormless and he gave a shrug.

'Oh God!' Jodie sighed in exasperation, as if Fred was somehow letting her down personally. 'Ring him and ask, Fred!' she urged.

'He's out,' said Fred furtively, 'all day.'

'My mum might be able to find out,' Jess said bravely. 'The paperwork's in my bedroom . . .' A few scrappy notes were all the 'paperwork' that existed.

'Ring her now!' commanded Jodie.

Jess's blood boiled. How dare Jodie start acting as if this was her event and Jess was some kind of servant! Under the table, Jess secretly dug her finger-nails into her palms to avoid letting fly with a stinging blow across Jodie's chops. Her only comfort now was that Jodie's spots were even worse than her own. But in a way Jodie was right. How could they organise the buffet without knowing all this tiresome stuff and doing some sums? Thank God Flora was by her side.

Jess got out her phone and discovered there was a text waiting, coincidentally, from Mum herself.

GUESS WHAT! HAVE MET HALF-GORGEOUS MAN CALLED MARTIN. CURRENTLY LUNCHING AT ALFREDO'S. HE MIGHT

Jess's brain reeled. In the midst of her Chaos crisis, Mum had to go off on some kind of romantic escapade. This was giving Jess a headache.

'She's not at home right now.' Jess shrugged and pocketed her phone again.

'How do you know?' yelled Jodie, slapping her head as if Jess was a complete idiot.

Jess ignored her. She wasn't going to tell Jodie about her mum's romantic entanglements. There was a brief pause.

Fred stirred in his chair. 'And, of course, once we've organised the buffet,' he murmured, with a sly subversive grin, 'don't forget we need chandeliers, fountains, lasers, a flock of white doves . . .'

'Shut up, Fred!' snapped Jess. This was so not the time for stupid irrelevant jokes. How could he be like this, knowing what deep trouble they were in?

'So this buffet,' drawled Tiffany, yawning. 'What are you going to have?'

'I've seen some great menus on the internet,' said Jodie with a self-important toss of the head. 'Get this: prawn fritters, filet mignon, or a veggie and cheese pancake for vegetarians.'

'I want lasagne!' said Mackenzie. 'Filet mignon – that's steak, right? You're talking big bucks. Plus, I hate prawns – they're gross, like goddam insects.'

'How do you make fritters?' asked Ben Jones. 'Don't you have to, uh, like, deep-fry them?'

'Yeah, of course. Why?' demanded Jodie.

'Have you got a deep-fat fryer?' asked Tiffany. 'My dad's a junk-food addict – maybe you could borrow his.'

'There should be one in the kitchen,' said Mackenzie, frowning.

'What kitchen?' asked Ben Jones. 'Sorry to be a bit thick.'

'The kitchen of the venue where we're holding it, dummy!' grinned Mackenzie. (He often talked like that to Ben.)

'So does St Mark's Church Hall have a deep-fat fryer?' asked Ben.

'Never mind the prawn fritters, then!' exploded Jodie. 'We can have something simpler!'

'Why simpler?' muttered Fred, still staring at the ceiling. 'Why not Indonesian stir-fry? Why not roast swan?'

'I don't think we should try and do the catering ourselves!' Flora interrupted nervously. 'I think Jess and Fred were planning to get caterers in, right?' She turned to Jess, for whom the whole concept of caterers was welcome, novel and also terrifying.

'Yeah, caterers,' Jess croaked.

'Who's doing it, then?' demanded Jodie.

'I haven't decided yet,' murmured Jess, feeling faint.

'Who have you spoken to?' asked Mackenzie. 'Ask them how much it would be for lasagne. Everybody likes lasagne. And it's cheap.'

Jess was silent. By now, obviously, she should have worked out what the budget was, spoken to heaps of caterers, got quotes from them and discussed menus. Above all, she should have opened a bank account and stashed all the money safely away in it. Instead of all the big important stuff, she had just let life roll along as usual, playing Scrabble with Mum, watching *The X Files* with Fred and wasting hours discussing their stand-up routine.

Just then Beast Hawkins and some other rugby guys burst into the Dolphin.

'Rugby match in twenty minutes!' he boomed. 'Ashcroft Pumas versus Christchurch Colts! Come on, guys – we need support!'

Jodie scrambled to her feet, followed by Tiffany,

Mackenzie and Ben Jones, for whom sport was something of a religion. Flora also got up and then turned to Jess with a kind of apologetic cringe.

'I promised Jack I'd meet him there,' she said. 'I ought to go . . . Don't worry, guys, it'll all be fine. Catch you later, OK?' Then she was gone – everyone was gone, and Jess and Fred were left alone together in an atmosphere of dust, ashes and ruins.

Chapter 14

Suddenly Maria turned the music up; evidently she was going through an emotional patch. She marched to their table and cleared all the coffee cups.

'Are you having lunch?' she demanded moodily. The unspoken message was: '*Order some food or clear out*'. One of the charms of the Dolphin Cafe was the mercurial charisma of Maria, who had a passionate, Mediterranean temperament and occasionally threw china if one of her beaux let her down.

'Let's eat!' Jess shouted above the music. 'We might as well! I'm starving now!'

Fred nodded and did the honours; he queued for a panini and brought a plate of nachos for Jess. A big power ballad was blasting from the sound system – always a sign that Maria was on a downer.

'So,' said Fred perkily, 'Chaos – The Never-ending

Story. How shall we play the hosting thing? In character? In fancy dress?'

Jess couldn't believe it. Fred was still obsessing about the hosting stuff, when they hadn't got any further with the music or the food or, most importantly of all, the money. Of course, they did also need to get their act together – literally. Jess had tried to think of some fun ways of hosting the event, but she'd never managed to concentrate properly – she'd been snowed under with all the other stuff.

'Fred!' yelled Jess. 'Never mind the hosting bit! Where's the goddam money? And what are we going to do about the food or the music?' She scooped some sour cream and guacamole on to her first nacho and raised it to her lips.

'Ah, the money,' he said in an offhand way. 'Maybe you should –' Fred started to talk, but the cappuccino machine kicked in with its deafening blast of steam.

Though Fred was talking to her, he wasn't looking at her. His eyes were roving over the whole room and Jess couldn't help feeling that this symbolised Fred's failure to focus on the problems they faced, starting with his refusal to accept that the money was definitely under his bed, because she knew for a fact it wasn't under hers.

Something horrid happened to the nacho in her mouth – it turned to leather, the sour cream curdled into some kind of horrible scum, and the guacamole became engine oil. It wasn't the Dolphin Cafe's fault – their nachos were, if not sublime, at least always very tasty. Jess forced it down with a gigantic swig of cola (another new year's resolution gone!) and then began to wonder what would happen to the enormous ball of gas she seemed to have swallowed. Abruptly the cappuccino machine finished its noise.

'I didn't hear a word of anything you said then,' said Jess loudly, watching in faint disgust as Fred shoved a huge bit of panini into his mouth.

He then went off into a comedy routine about trying to talk with his mouth full: 'Ommmggg umggggh ughmmmm gummity gummity gummmngh . . .'

Jess felt anguished. Fred seemed so completely oblivious to the turmoil she was in. His clowning about might have been amusing once, but for the first time in her life, Jess was not finding Fred funny. The ball of gas Jess had swallowed had somehow turned into a heavy sack of poison that was hanging down inside her.

Desperate to escape into something, Jess tore into

the next nacho. She wasn't going to be beaten by a plate of corn chips; she forced them down relentlessly, like a garbage lorry swallowing black plastic sacks, only with rather less enjoyment. Fred was still talking, but, it seemed, more *at* her than *to* her. She recognised the expression on his face – it was the way he looked when he was endlessly flannelling, the way he looked when spinning loads of yarns to a teacher whose homework he had somehow neglected to complete. How had she turned into a teacher for Fred? Where was their old effortless understanding? This was horribly wrong. Suddenly the power ballad finished its dramatic climax.

'Look,' said Fred in the sudden silence, 'if you organise the food and the music, I'll write the script. How about that?'

'Fred!' yelled Jess. 'I keep telling you! Chaos will be fine without our stand-up routine, but if there's no food and no music, people will go mental and we'll be famous till the end of time for our crap event! Plus Oxfam will get nothing and all those starving kids we should have helped will still be desperate! That was why we wanted to organise this in the first place, remember? To help those poor little kids in Africa, where they've had that terrible drought and there's literally no food! Now listen – *no way* can I organise everything! You're being totally unhelpful and annoying. The first thing you've got to do is find the money!'

'I've looked, honest,' said Fred hurriedly. 'It's definitely not in my bedroom.'

'It must be!' raged Jess. 'Look again!'

'All right, all right!' Fred looked really uneasy. 'I'll look again! And I'll organise the music!'

'Well, make sure you do!' Jess was feeling terrible now, both furious with Fred and sick because of the nachos she'd stuffed in her face. She hated the nagging teacherish person she seemed to have become, but was seized with dread at the feeling that Chaos would never get organised. It would be a five-star fiasco.

'I'm going,' said Jess suddenly, lurching to her feet. 'I've got to try and do something about the catering stuff.'

She was faintly aware of Fred looking up, startled, but not getting up, as she pushed past him, angrily heading for the door, and burst out into the street.

Snowflakes were spiralling down. It could have been a magical moment, but the boy who would have made it magic was back there in the cafe, stuffing his face with panini, and he evidently didn't care enough about her to come rushing after her to find out what was wrong.

A lorryload of nachos washed down with a vat of cola was one thing that was wrong, for a start. Jess paused and rubbed her tum. *Waaaaaaarp!* A deafening burp exploded from her mouth just as two college boys were passing by.

'Charming!' said the tall guy.

Jess didn't care – so what if people found her disgusting? She was full of toxic things – not just the nachos, but everything that had happened today.

Jess pretended to look in her bag for something, to give her an excuse to loiter, just in case Fred had bolted the last of his panini and was scrambling after her. But the door of the cafe remained firmly closed.

Jess embarked on a long trawl of the town centre. She went into restaurant after restaurant (plenty of them opened for Sunday lunch) and pub after pub, asking if they did outside catering, and received absolutely no encouragement whatsoever. Nobody seemed to want to take on her event. Everybody had organised their own Valentine's evening *months* ago. Jess finally gave up after the thirteenth snooty refusal and escaped out on to the pavement, which was covered in slush. The snow had stopped and been replaced with tiny little daggers of icy rain. It seemed as if the whole universe was against her.

Jess walked briskly home. This was partly to keep warm, partly to stop herself from crying, and partly to try and get her tummy feeling right again – there was an explosive quality to her digestion right now which was a bit unnerving. Though the day had been one of the worst ever, she would quite like to make it back home without vomming in the street – avoiding that would count, right now, as some kind of triumph.

Chapter 15

As Jess trailed wearily up the front path, she tried to summon up the energy to look positive and confident for Mum and Granny. They mustn't know what a dire mess she was in. Her mind was racing with a thousand contradictory thoughts: one moment she felt furious with Fred, the next she felt it was all her fault and it was stupid to expect Fred to be able to organise anything. Her eyes filled with tears. She had half a mind to let rip with a massive crying fit – Mum and Granny would be sympathetic, and would make some lovely treats for her (maybe Granny would dig deep and even serve up some delicious cranberry muffins).

But as Jess opened the door, an unexpected sound met her ears. A stranger's voice – a man's voice – was coming out of the kitchen: '. . . Ten, plus it's a double-letter score, so that's twenty, uh, forty-six, I think.'

'Dammit!' That was Mum's voice, but sounding oddly deranged, as if she was performing in a play. 'You're so sneaky! I was saving up a certain something for that!'

'A certain Z, I presume? Tough, baby.'

Ugh! They were playing Scrabble – in pretend American accents. This must be the famous half-gorgeous Martin. Jess's heart plummeted right through the hall carpet. This was all she needed. She'd come home angsty and traumatised, and now she had to be polite to some dork who had wormed his way into Mum's affections while her back was turned and who didn't have the courtesy to lose to her at Scrabble.

The sound of the TV echoed from the sitting room. Jess assumed Granny was in there, and, after closing the front door very quietly, she tiptoed in. Granny was fast asleep in front of *The Antiques Roadshow*. 'This is a quite wonderful, charming little piece,' the jewellery man was saying, his fingers, in massive close-up, trembling slightly as he showed a tiny brooch to the camera. 'And you know, it's all about the symbolism of love. It's a very romantic object which could have been given to a young lady by her sweetheart on the occasion of their engagement, or possibly on Saint Valentine's Day.'

All this Valentine's stuff was too much – tears burst from Jess's eyes, and she ran upstairs and locked herself in the bathroom. She turned the bath taps on and pulled her clothes off, sobbing occasionally but looking forward to a long, hot, steamy, therapeutic soak. But something wasn't quite right – where were the clouds of inviting steam that should be billowing out? Gingerly she reached out and touched the water: it was stone cold. God, this house! Why did nothing ever work properly?

'Jess?' And now there was Mum out on the landing, pestering her!

'What?' Jess was so exasperated now that she stopped crying and started to feel murderous instead. She preferred it, on the whole.

'What are you doing, love?'

'Well, I'd be having a bath if there was any hot water available in this useless house, but instead I'm getting dressed again!' snapped Jess.

'Sorry, I forgot to switch the immersion on when we got in. What's wrong, Jess? How was your day?'

For a moment Jess was so, so tempted to confess

what a deep, soggy, stinking mess she was in. 'It was fine,' she lied instead. She couldn't let herself get upset now with this Martin person in the house.

'Oh good! Come downstairs and meet Martin. He's lovely – you'll love him,' Mum prattled on in a confident way which Jess found deeply irritating, though under the irritation Jess knew she ought to be happy for her mum that, at last, she'd met a man who was halfway human. 'We saved some cottage pie for you and it's still warm in the oven.' After delivering this interesting piece of news, Mum could be heard going downstairs.

Jess sat on the end of the bath, pulling on her socks and having a think. That cottage pie was calling to her suddenly, all warm and savoury and slightly crusty, the way things are when they've been waiting in the oven. It doesn't suit some things but it certainly suits cottage pie. Jess's mouth began to water – it was a big improvement on the eyes watering a few minutes ago. She stood up, wriggled into her boots and pulled her jumper down. A brief look in the mirror assured her that, though pale and preoccupied, she didn't look too weird or mad, and besides, however nice the half-gorgeous Martin was, she basically didn't give a flying fandango whether he thought she looked weird or not.

So, moments later, Jess marched into the kitchen. Mum and Martin were sitting at the kitchen table with a Scrabble board laid out between them. Martin turned round in his chair and looked up at Jess. He had short brown hair, a wide, open, friendly face and large, twinkly eyes.

'Martin, this is Jess,' said Mum, looking pleased that Jess had come down. Martin scrambled clumsily to his feet and held out his hand; he was tall and rangy.

'Hello,' he said with a friendly smile. 'How very nice to meet you!' He had a proper handshake and he seemed kind of energetic and well-meaning. Jess began to be ashamed that she hadn't wanted to meet him.

'Jess has spent today organising a dinner dance,' said Mum, also getting up. 'It's in aid of Oxfam. I'll get your supper out, love.'

'A dinner dance? Wow!' said Martin, pushing the Scrabble board aside. 'Tell us about it.'

Jess was annoyed with her mum for mentioning Chaos and Martin's eager smile and sympathetic manner made things worse. But the smell of cottage pie was truly divine and Jess started to feel ravenous.

She must have walked for hours up and down the town centre, looking for caterers.

'Oh, it's really boring.' Jess took a deep breath, picked up her fork and tasted the first mouthful of cottage pie. It was delicious. 'Mum, this is great. Thanks.'

'Jess likes organising things,' Mum went on, foolishly boasting. If only she knew. 'Last Christmas she and her boyfriend Fred put on a wonderful comedy show in school and raised loads of money for charity.'

'Amazing!' said Martin. 'What's Fred like?'

'He's hilarious!' said Mum, beaming. Jess was annoyed that, at the very moment when she was totally furious with Fred, Mum had somehow become his PR officer.

'He is funny.' Jess had to agree. This was not the time or place for an anti-Fred rant. She had to swallow her rage with him. It wouldn't be appropriate to let rip now, in front of Martin. 'He's kind of shy, but he hides it with jokes and stuff,' she admitted between clenched teeth. 'The Christmas show was basically Fred's idea – he inspired the whole thing, wrote it and directed it.' It was inconvenient, right now, to remind herself of just how talented Fred was.

'Did he?' asked Martin, his big eyes kind of

expanding in surprise and admiration. 'That must have been amazing. Tell me about it!'

So Jess told him all about the Christmas show while she ate her cottage pie, and after about twenty minutes somehow she felt almost herself again. Martin was indeed lovely – he seemed genuinely interested in everything, and had really tuned in to the kind of guy Fred was. In fact, what he'd said had revived her sympathy for Fred. She began to believe that everything was going to be all right after all.

Maybe, this time, Mum really had struck gold. She'd only known Martin for a few hours at most, but already Jess was starting to think that if she had to have a stepfather, Martin would be a very sweet and friendly one.

Then the doorbell rang.

Jess jumped up – she assumed it was Fred, and raced to the door because she couldn't wait to welcome him and assure him that everything was fine, she totally understood and there was no need to worry. She flung the door open, and there, in the frosty lamplight, stood Dad, carrying two cases. He gave her a doleful, tragic and self-pitying look.

'My life,' he said, 'is in ruins.'

Chapter 16

'Dad!' squeaked Jess in shock. 'What are you doing here? What do you mean, your life's in ruins?'

'Aren't you going to ask me in?' said Dad in a wheedling kind of voice. 'I've just come all the way up from Cornwall on the coach because I couldn't afford the train and I haven't slept properly for a week and I'm almost hallucinating.'

'Of course! Right!' Jess stood aside to let her dad in, though her mind was racing. Any minute now he was going to see Mum friskily enjoying a game of Scrabble with another man behind his back. OK, he and Mum had been divorced for fourteen years, but it still might be a particularly upsetting hallucination for him, and in his present state, it might push Dad right over the edge.

And what might it do to Mum and Martin? They

were getting along so well, and the atmosphere had been so merry that even Jess's black mood had vanished. Why did Dad have to burst in now, all needy and panicky, at this most inconvenient of moments?

Jess hesitated. 'Maybe, er . . . Granny's watching TV in here, I think . . .'

But Dad ignored the idea of Granny – he could obviously hear Mum laughing rather skittishly in the kitchen. 'But Mum's in the kitchen,' he said, dumping both his cases in the hall and just barging through.

Jess followed him hastily, biting her nails in anxiety and wishing she could have warned Mum. But it was too late. She saw the moment when Mum looked up from her Scrabble and tried to get to grips with the mysterious and puzzling fact that her ex had appeared. Every tiny scrap of fun faded from Mum's face, and so did the faintest hint of colour; it simply drained away. One moment she was rosy and pink, the next she was pale and astonished like somebody who had seen a ghost.

'T-Tim?' she faltered. 'What's going on?'

'My life is in ruins,' said Dad again. Jess was really irritated that he'd said that without being introduced to Martin or anything. Of course, she was really sorry to hear her dad was upset and stuff, and she obviously loved him more than anyone else in the world apart from Mum and Granny and Fred, but really, did Dad have to come over all melodramatic in front of a total stranger?

Martin stared up at him in amazement and shock.

'Sorry.' Dad appeared to realise his entrance had been a tad over the top. 'I'm Tim Jordan.'

Martin got up and extended his hand.

'Tim's my ex,' added Mum, trying to keep exasperation and a thousand other emotions out of her voice. 'Tim, this is Martin. Martin Davies.'

'Ah!' said Martin, keeping it light and obviously hoping to avoid any unpleasantness. 'I thought you lived in Cornwall.'

'So did I,' Dad said gloomily and bitterly. He slumped into the nearest chair, which had been Jess's.

'What's happened, Tim?' asked Mum, retreating towards the kettle. 'Can I get you some tea?'

'Wouldn't mind something stronger,' said Dad, looking jealously at the wine glasses.

Jess watched, mesmerised. What was all this about? For the past couple of years she'd been boasting about how her glamorous gay artist dad lived in a fabulous big white house by the sea in St Ives with a designer and boutique owner called Phil, who was a champion surfer when he wasn't wearing gold lamé socks.

'Help us finish this bottle, then,' said Mum with a hint of irritation, pouring Dad a glass of white wine.

Martin looked uncertain whether to stay or go; he rubbed his face and took a furtive peep at his watch.

'Thanks, thanks,' said Dad. 'I hate to ask, I hate to behave like this. I'm being a total wimp, I know, but do you have anything to eat? I haven't eaten since breakfast.'

Suddenly Martin got up. 'Uh, maybe it's time I was getting along,' he murmured.

'Oh, don't leave now, Martin!' cried Mum in dismay. 'Tim won't be here long. I'll just make you a cheese sandwich, Tim,' she went on swiftly, with a steely tone entering her voice. 'Sit down, Martin, and have another glass of wine.'

Martin obeyed.

'What's happened, Dad?' asked Jess.

'Well.' Dad heaved a big sigh and started sipping his wine. 'It's – Phil decided he wanted to move to Barcelona. His business has been struggling a bit since the economic downturn, you know.'

'Oh dear,' said Mum anxiously.

'So he's decided to sell his business, and the

house, of course – and believe it or not, somebody snapped the house up within a week of it going on the market.'

'No!' gasped Jess. That lovely house! With its white walls and its blue glass and the sound of seagulls wheeling on the wind outside! Her favourite bolt-hole and home from home! Dad looked guiltily at her.

'Sorry, love,' he said.

'So what's your share?' demanded Mum, starting to sound a bit tense and cold. She'd always hated things being out of control. Recently she'd lightened up a little and fun had been creeping back into her life, but with Dad's news it was almost as if she'd had to strap her armour on again, like a knight going into the battle.

'My share? Nothing,' replied Dad. 'Well, virtually nothing. It was always Phil's house – I mean, he's a successful businessman. I'm an unsuccessful artist, as you know.' He did a strange lame little shrug. 'I didn't want to move to Barcelona. Obviously because of Jess, mainly.' Jess felt strangely guilty just for existing. 'But also there were other issues . . . It's hard when you're financially dependent on somebody . . . It was OK at first, but it hasn't really been working for some time . . .'

Jess suddenly remembered how Phil had been a bit preoccupied when she'd phoned – not quite as friendly as usual. Maybe he and Dad had had a row that evening.

'So . . . that's it, I'm afraid. Curtains.' Dad's voice trailed miserably away, the kettle boiled and Martin suddenly seemed to reach a decision, leaping to his feet and grabbing his coat.

'I'll be off, I think,' he said in an embarrassed voice. Jess felt sorry for him. 'You've obviously got a lot to talk about. Nice to meet you, Jess, Tim. Give my best to your mum, Madeleine . . .' He hesitated, and there was an awful moment during which everyone waited to see whether he was going to kiss Mum goodbye. Even a totally sexless peck on the cheek would have been appalling in the circumstances. Thank God Martin did the decent thing and backed off hastily towards the door, dispensing twinkly but anxious smiles in all directions. 'I'll let myself out,' he said, and he did.

Mum stood, holding the kettle, throughout his entire exit, seemingly frozen or paralysed like somebody in a fairytale. Little wafts of steam floated up out of the kettle's spout, making the tiny hairs around her brow wave slightly, as if they were waving goodbye.

'Congratulations, Dad!' snapped Jess, as the front door slammed shut behind Martin. 'You've just ruined the first decent date Mum has had since – well, for ages.' It would be best not to mention last year's Japanese toy boy.

'What?' Dad seemed lost in a mist. 'Who . . . who was that again?'

'He was Mum's date,' said Jess sternly. 'A lovely guy called Martin.'

'Oh God!' Dad clapped his hand across his mouth like a naughty schoolboy. 'I'm so sorry, Madeleine.'

'Don't worry. It's nothing. He wasn't a date really, anyway,' said Mum irritably, fussing and fretting with bread and cheese, and pretending like mad that it really didn't matter, even though it was obvious it mattered like hell.

'But I kind of turned up here as if . . . as if –'

'No, you didn't,' said Mum bleakly. 'As if nothing. There is no As If.'

'But I've ruined everything for you!' wailed Dad. 'Again!'

'Shut up. Don't be silly,' said Mum. 'I'm having a coffee – would you like one? A decaf?'

'Thanks, no – yes – I don't know,' said Dad helplessly, dropping his head into his hands.

'Have a coffee,' said Mum, slapping the sandwich down in front of him like a cafe owner who is longing to close the shop. 'It'll keep you going till you get to wherever it is you're staying. Where are you staying, anyway?'

Dad hesitated for a split second, looking pale, tragic and ever so slightly apologetic. 'Uhhhh, I haven't got anywhere,' he murmured guiltily. 'I'm so sorry, Madeleine – could I possibly doss down on your sofa for the night?'

Mum stared at him blankly for a moment, then she seemed to shake herself and get her focus back. 'Of course,' she said briskly. Jess could tell she was furious. 'Except you can't possibly sleep on the sofa. You can have Jess's room and Jess can come in with me.'

Jess felt a spear of resentment. Why did Dad have to have her room? Why couldn't he sleep on the sofa? He was behaving a bit like a teenager, so why couldn't he sleep like one? She was tempted to object, but it so obviously wouldn't help, and she felt very sorry for Mum, whose brave new world had crashed and burned in one short quarter of an hour.

There was the sound of somebody coming along the hall – it was Granny, who had slept through the

131

whole drama. She entered and screwed up her eyes slightly. It had been dark as she snoozed in the sitting room, with just the low lamps and the TV's flicker.

'I heard the front door go, Madeleine,' she muttered blearily, still half asleep. 'Is Jess back safely? How are you getting on with the Scrabble, Martin? Oh! You're not Martin. Oh my God! You're Tim!' Granny was suddenly wide awake, and who could blame her?

At bedtime Jess received a text from Fred. **BAND FIXED UP – FRENZY. THAT'S THEIR NAME BUT ALSO MY STATE OF MIND. SORRY I WAS A BIT WEIRD IN THE CAFE. LOW BLOOD SUGAR.**

Jess heaved a huge, huge sigh. So they had a band! Things were looking up – at last one thing was going right. Now the priority was finding the money. She whizzed him a reply. **WELL DONE FOR FINDING FRENZY! BUT WHAT ABOUT THE MUNS? HAVE YOU LOOKED UNDER YOUR BED YET?**

Chapter 17

Next morning on the way to school, Jess brought Flora up to date on her useless Dad's unscheduled arrival.

'Basically, I think he's ruined Mum's best chance of finding somebody really nice,' Jess concluded. 'Martin was a lovely guy, but he's not going to want to get involved with somebody whose ex has just turned up and moved in, is he?'

'Maybe he will,' said Flora uncertainly. 'If he really likes her, he'll at least want to find out what the score is between your dad and your mum – I mean, they're not exactly old flames, are they?'

'No,' agreed Jess. 'Even when they were young, they won the Nobel Prize for Least Amorous Couple. But Martin doesn't know that.'

'Maybe he does,' mused Flora. 'Maybe your mum's told him.'

They were nearing the school gates now, and Jess's attention began to ebb away from the parental saga to the much more urgent and gripping issue of where Fred was and whether he'd found the money. If he insisted he hadn't got a clue where it was, she hoped she'd be able to remain smiling and gracious as she ripped his head from his body and booted it over the science block.

Ah, there was Fred! A tiny explosion of hope fizzed up through her ribcage and soared up to her head, where it caused her ear lobes to vibrate. Fred was standing on the edge of a group that included Jodie, Ben Jones, Mackenzie, Tiffany, and Zoe Morris and Chloe Thingummyjig from the year below. She couldn't tell by his body language what kind of mood he was in.

Obviously she couldn't mention the money with everybody standing there. Maybe Fred was hiding in crowds because he knew she couldn't confront him in public. He was such a coward. Though Fred seemed engrossed in what Mackenzie was saying, Jodie beckoned them over with an infectious grin.

'Jess! Flo! Come here and listen to Mackenzie doing a Wayne Rooney!' Jodie bawled.

Fred turned towards her and Jess waited for a sign

from him that things were OK. But somehow he seemed to fix his gaze on Flora instead, hesitating, his mouth half open, a quizzical frown hovering above his elusive grey eyes.

At this point the bell rang, and they trooped towards the door. Jess managed to position herself alongside Fred. They weren't alone, but it was the next best thing.

'Great about the band!' she whispered. 'But have you found the muns?'

'I keep telling you.' Fred turned and stared into her face for a split second, his eyes wide and panicky. '*You* had it!'

'But I've turned my room completely upside down!' insisted Jess, her pulse racing. 'There's no sign of it! I know I did have it for the first few weeks, but then you took it – I'm sure.'

'I did have some of it for a while,' admitted Fred. 'But then I gave it to you with all the paperwork – don't you remember?' He still looked jittery, though. Jess's panic spiralled downwards. Her heart was hammering away like mad. What if they never found it? They'd have to cancel the whole thing and spend the rest of their lives working to pay people their money back. Oh God! She would never organise anything ever again. It was misery.

After all that, the French test was almost a blessed relief. For the rest of the day, Jess hardly had a chance to speak to Fred at all. At break she was in detention (history homework had caught up with her at last); at lunchtime Fred had yet more infuriating Chess Club practice, and after school he had to go off with Mr Dickson and the chess team because there was a match against St Benedict's. Honestly! Why couldn't he put the dinner dance first, just for a few days? Jess hadn't had a chance even for a brief moment of shared hysteria.

She packed her bag with a heavy heart (not literally – she wasn't into offal) and, sighing, wrapped her fave stripy scarf around her throat. It was another dark, frosty afternoon.

'Come on,' said Flora. 'Let's go to Jack's.' Jack had left school early for a dental appointment. 'He's texted me to say his face is still numb and he wants some TLC.'

'Blokes are such wimps,' sighed Jess. 'Anyway, I should go home really.'

'Just come for a few minutes,' urged Flora. 'It's on your way. You'll love Jack's house. It's amazing, but in a kind of unusual way. And it would be good for you to meet his mum before we go to Dorset.'

'OK.' Jess, though tormented, was still clinging on to the basics of politeness. Besides, she rather liked the idea of not going home right away – since Dad had arrived, there had been An Atmosphere. He hadn't revealed his plans for what to do next, and it seemed he might be camping out in her bedroom for some time.

Normally Jess went home, ran upstairs, dived into her lovely welcoming chaotic den, flung her bag in the corner and jumped on to the bed with her teddy and her laptop. Not having her own room waiting for her made her feel a bit like a refugee – she wouldn't be able to escape from Mum and Granny and, much as she loved them, she realised that having her own private space was essential to her sanity.

'So did you get a chance to talk to Fred?' asked Flora gently as they set off through the frosty white twinkling streets. 'Has he got a band organised?'

'Well,' said Jess cautiously, 'he *said* he's fixed up a band at last – Frenzy, apparently.' She still hadn't told Flora about the missing money, because it seemed so completely and utterly lame.

'Oh, that's great,' said Flora. 'I'm sure they'll be terrific! Plus there's always the DJ and the disco!

Cheer up, babe – it's going to be brilliant!'

'I know, I know!' said Jess, trying to shake off her secret angst about the missing money. 'Sorry to be such a moody cow.'

'The Moody Cow!' repeated Flora, with a nervous trying-too-hard kind of smile. 'Sounds like a pub. Maybe we should run a pub when we've left school.'

'Maybe,' said Jess listlessly. It was hard to join in the joke – she was so anxious, she felt as if she'd drunk a whole barrelful of icy water.

'Jack's house is along here,' said Flora, turning into a street of big terraced Georgian houses like in a Jane Austen movie. The door was dark green with a gleaming brass knocker shaped like a pineapple.

'I don't think I'll come in,' said Jess, beginning to back away. But then a blonde middle-aged woman, evidently Jack's mum, opened the door and flung her arms wide.

'Flora!' she trilled, embracing her.

'This is Jess,' said Flora shyly.

'Jess! How lovely to meet you! I'm so glad you're coming down to Dorset with us next weekend! Come in! Come in! Have some tea!' She hustled them indoors. 'Jack!' she called upstairs. 'Jack! Flora and Jess are here!' There was a muffled reply from upstairs.

'Come through to the kitchen and get warm!' Mrs Stevens went on. 'Gubbins will be thrilled to see you!' Jess wondered who Gubbins was. Although Jack's family seemed to be incredibly rich, she wasn't sure they had a butler.

The kitchen was a long room sort of tacked on at the back of the house. There was a huge cream range cooker with tea towels hanging from its bar, French windows showing a wintry garden of clipped evergreen shrubs and a starry tree that seemed to be flowering even in January, and a huge table strewn with cookery debris. Above the table there was a big window in the ceiling so you could look up and see the sky.

A little Jack Russell terrier leapt out of his basket, did a couple of growly excited barks and flew to greet the girls, jumping up and wagging his tail. At the same time Jack arrived.

'Hello, Jeff,' he said, smiling lopsidedly at Jess. 'I can't talk properly so I'm afraid you'll have to have a fex-change.'

'Hello, Gubbins!' Flora picked him up and he thrashed his tail wildly, licking her face in the most tickly way. 'Don't go mental, you naughty pup!' she gasped. 'Oh! My mascara!' She burst into uncontrollable giggles and passed him to Jack.

'Gubbins is a lovely name!' said Jess, rubbing the pup's tummy. 'I think I'll be a little old spinster one day with a terrier and some knitting.'

'You won't be a spinster!' beamed Mrs Stevens. 'The chaps will be fighting over you, young lady! And how is the lovely Fred? I'm dying to meet him.'

'The lovely Fred is at a chess match,' said Jess lightly, not wishing to go into the details of her present delirious happiness. 'Your kitchen is lovely – so cosy!'

'It's a great room for parties,' said Mrs Stevens. 'But not as good as our house in Dorset. In fact, we're having a little lunch party down there on the Sunday – it's our wedding anniversary. Nothing special, just roast beef and apple pie and then possibly charades around the fire. I've heard how brilliant you and Fred are at charades, Jess. I can't wait to see you perform!'

Chapter 18

As she arrived home and closed the front door behind her, Jess could hear her mum moving about in the kitchen, and she could tell by the way she was clattering the plates that her mood wasn't good. Had she heard from Martin today? Or had he vanished at the first hint of a challenge? Was Dad moving back in? Were they a family again? Jess rather hoped not. Things had been just fine as they were. This was all so disturbing. And it had been a bit of a shock to realise that Dad's beautiful house by the sea didn't actually belong to him.

Dad peered out of the kitchen door, smiled delightedly to see her, and came out and gave her a hug. 'I've made a fish pie!' he announced breezily. 'Of course, the fish can't compare with what I used to get in St Ives. But I did my best.'

'I'm sure it'll be delish!' Jess assured him. 'It smells great!'

'The fish you buy in St Ives has been caught literally a few hours before,' mused Dad with a faraway look – about two hundred miles far away. 'You can't get any fresher.'

'Yeah, yeah, spare us the commercial break,' said Jess, moving towards the kitchen.

Her dad remained in the hall for a moment, fondly remembering an eel he had once bought.

Mum was unloading the dishwasher with a bad-tempered frown. Speedily Jess cosied up to her and gave her a kiss.

'Have you heard from Martin?' she whispered urgently.

'No,' said Mum, trying to sound as if it hadn't crossed her mind as a possibility.

'The fish pie smells nice.' Jess tried to cheer her up.

'I don't particularly like fish pie,' said Mum, giving Jess a fishy stare.

'OK, well, never mind. I'll just go up and change,' said Jess, fantasizing about soft, warm jog-pants instead of school uniform, 'and maybe do my homework.'

'There's no time for homework now,' said Mum. Jess stared in amazement. This was the first and probably the only time this sentence would ever pass Mum's lips. 'Apparently this fish pie has to be eaten right now or it'll be ruined.' Mum looked a little exasperated. Jess felt sympathetic, but she hoped she would manage to stay positive. Dad would probably move on in a day or two.

'Well, I'll just go up and get changed at least,' said Jess. 'I'm in the mood for pyjamas or something cosy.'

She raced upstairs, but when she stepped inside her room, her tummy somersaulted with shock. Dad had tidied her room! All her papers had been gathered up off her desk, which was now shiny and organised. Where were those precious papers? They'd included a sketch of Mr Fothergill the English teacher morphing into an elephant, plus a very amusing dialogue about octopuses having sex, which she and Flora had secretly written in the French lesson when they should have been doing their translations. And the floor – it was visible! All her clothes had been picked up and hung in the wardrobe, or even, who knows, possibly folded up and put away in the drawers . . . She would never be able to find her stuff again.

It was bad enough that her suddenly homeless dad should move into her bedroom so she had to share with mum – who read novels half the night, by the way, keeping Jess awake; bad enough that he should show no signs so far of moving on or moving out. But to tidy her room behind her back? That was a crime against humanity! Jess was fuming.

He'd had all day to pick over her personal stuff, read her private notes even – Jess's heart gave a terrible lurch – devour her diary, which she noticed was tidily placed on her bedside table. He'd definitely touched it, then – it normally lived under her pillow. Oh God!

Jess ran from her room in disgust, thundered downstairs and burst into the kitchen, spitting venom. Dad was straining some peas and Mum was laying the table. They both looked up in alarm at Jess's dramatic entrance.

'Dad!' she screamed. 'You've tidied my room! You've been messing about with all my private stuff! That's so totally out of order! How could you?'

Some strange expressions flitted across Dad's face. He shared a quick glance with Mum.

'Sorry about that,' he said, his tone strangely light-hearted. 'But maybe you should find somewhere a little safer for this.' He picked up a big bulging envelope from the dresser and held it out. Jess's heart gave a leap. She grabbed the envelope and peered inside – it was the money! A big sheaf of cheques and bundles of cash! She flung herself gratefully into Dad's arms.

'Oh Dad! You're such a legend! Sorry I was in a strop about the tidying! Where did you find it?'

'Down the back of your desk – between the desk and the wall,' said Dad. 'I couldn't quite work out whether you'd put it there deliberately, or if it had just dropped down.'

'You *must* open an account and put it all in the bank!' scolded Mum. 'How have you managed to pay for everything?'

'Don't worry, Muv, it's all under control!' trilled Jess. Clutching the magic envelope to her heart, she bolted back upstairs.

For a moment she hesitated on the landing. Should she text Fred and tell him the good news? The trouble was, she'd been quite hard on him, thinking he'd got the money, and all the time it had been in her bedroom. But then, Fred had been so annoyingly carefree about the whole thing . . . Jess decided to wait.

Carefully she placed the envelope on Mum's dressing table, because of course she was sharing Mum's room at the moment. It was hardly the chic lifestyle one hoped for at the age of sixteen, but finding the money had made Jess feel insanely cheerful. Pulling off her uniform, Jess plunged into her mum's collection of huge soft comfy clothing. Now, at last, she could relax!

She chose some grey jog-pants which looked as if they'd last been used by the inmate of a fat camp, a big man's shirt in a faded check, and a very old but comforting fleece with the zip half hanging off – the perfect outfit for her evening of cosy celebration. (Although she still hadn't sorted the problem of the catering, she was determined to shove it to the back of her mind for a couple of hours. She sometimes thought, in desperation, that if the worst came to the worst they could always order a huge delivery of ready meals and stuff from a supermarket.)

Halfway downstairs, she found a particularly tempting crispy bogey in her left nostril. She had a finger stuffed halfway up her nose and was sauntering down in her hideous garb, looking like something out of a horror movie, when the front door opened and Granny came in. She was always visiting her friend

Deborah these days. Maybe Granny could go and stay with her until Dad moved out – then he could have her room.

Granny turned round by the front door and said, 'Come in, then, dear. Jess'll be thrilled to see you!'

Jess froze and cringed back up a stair or two. Nobody must see her like this! She had literally never looked so gross. Who on earth . . . ?

Granny looked up the stairs. 'Ah, hello, love!' she crooned. 'Guess who I just met by the front gate?'

Jess braced herself, horrified that anyone was going to see her all dolled up in her mum's least attractive outfit. The person edged in through the front door. It was Fred.

He looked up with rather less rapture than Romeo gazing up at Juliet's balcony. It was impossible to read his mind. For a moment Jess felt kind of pinned to the stairs like a smelly old sock on a noticeboard; the fat-camp pants would look especially horrendous from below.

'Oh, hi!' said Jess, trying to sound casual but divine. 'How was the chess match?'

'Uh . . . hi,' replied Fred. 'Fine. We lost.'

At this moment Dad burst out of the kitchen, looking excited. 'Fred!' he exclaimed, charging down the hall and shaking hands ferociously with the poor guy. 'You must stay to supper! I've just made my signature fish pie! Phone home and tell 'em you'll be late!'

Jess wondered why Fred had come round – presumably it was something to do with the Chaos chaos. She knew he wouldn't mention anything in front of The Parents about the godawful mess they were in. She had to have a private word with him somehow or other, because she was longing to tell him that Dad had found the money – and of course, she owed Fred a huge apology for thinking he had lost it.

Dad and Fred were enjoying a flamboyant reunion: Dad was leaping about excitedly as if Fred was his son, or possibly stepson, or possibly . . . son-in-law. Fred was goofily gangling about as usual, but he had already been persuaded to part with his coat.

'OK, then – er, thanks,' he muttered, looking charmed but awkward.

Dear Fred! thought Jess. If only she wasn't bundled up like a street person! Jess slid down the last few stairs with what she hoped was graceful panache, but unfortunately the sleeve of the man's shirt she was wearing caught on the bottom of the banisters and forced her to leap backwards like a tethered dog with behavioural problems. Then she tried to cover her tracks by performing a kind of comic clowning staggering fit, but when she looked up, she realised that Fred had followed Dad into the kitchen, and her stupid antics had been for the benefit of Mr Nobody.

Chapter 19

'Come on, Fred – sit here!' Dad was turning into a manic master of ceremonies, settling Fred down opposite Jess and laying an extra place.

'Hello, Mrs Jordan,' said Fred warily. Mum nodded to him, giving a tight little smile. You could see she hated the way this evening was turning into some kind of gala. She was tired – Jess could always tell; there were little shadows at the corners of her eyes. She'd probably had a hard day dealing with shouty lunatics in the library.

'Right!' cried Dad with the air of a conjuror. 'Madeleine, pass me the magic oven gloves!' Mum obliged, with a weary look.

'Oooh, lovely!' said Granny excitedly, rubbing her hands. 'I love fish pie! Oh, there's no prawns in it, is there, Tim?'

'*Are* no prawns, plural,' Mum corrected her. She didn't usually comment on Granny's grammar – it was a sign she was in an irritable state of mind.

'No prawns, no sharks, no whales, and definitely no dolphins!' Dad promised. He threw the oven door open, bent down and pulled out the fish pie, which was a lovely golden colour and bubbling faintly at the edges.

'Is there cheese on top, Tim?' asked Granny.

'There is cheese on top!' Dad declared proudly. Then, ridiculously, he started to sing to the tune of some opera or other, 'Fish pie! Fish pie! Fish pie! Is there cheese on top? Cheese on top? On top? Oh yes, yes, yes, yes, yes! Tra-la!' He was over-compensating for Mum's gloominess. If only they could both just be normal and boring like other parents. Fred's dad, for example, would die rather than sing. Jess cringed in embarrassment and was tempted to slide under the table.

Dad picked up the serving spoon and Mum brought a pile of plates over. He had taken his place at the head of the table, where Mum usually sat. Jess felt he shouldn't have done it. But that was the least of her problems – for a start, she looked grotesque in her jog-pants and ragged fleece. And secondly, in less than two weeks she was going to have to feed nearly a hundred people . . . but no, she'd promised herself she wouldn't think about that tonight!

'I made a salad to go with it,' said Mum, 'as fish pie can be a bit fatty.' Jess wondered wildly if her parents could be persuaded to make a fish pie the size of a double bed and a salad as big as an allotment, enough to feed ninety-two, the Saturday after next.

'Don't you worry about fatty food, Mad!' Dad reassured Mum. He often called her Mad – ironically, really, as Mum had once confided to Jess that living with him had almost driven her stark staring bonkers. 'Fish oil is good oil – it's omega three or five or what-ever. Good for the heart!' He patted himself skittishly on the chest.

'What about the cheese, though?' nagged Mum.

'Well, scrape the cheese off and give it to Fred!' suggested Dad, doling out portions. Even though Jess was technically a bit overweight (she'd done the BMI quiz on the internet and everything), she was still annoyed with Dad for suggesting the extra cheese should go to Fred, not her. Whose dad was he, anyway?

'Would you like my cheese, Fred?' asked Mum.

Fred nodded eagerly. 'Yeah, please!' he said.

'Just a very small portion for me, please, Dad!' pleaded Jess urgently, but a massive slop of pie came her way.

'You're not too fat, honeybun!' Dad assured her, smiling charismatically and flicking a long lock of fair hair out of his eyes. 'You're perfect – isn't she, Fred?'

Fred looked startled and avoided her gaze. 'Oh, totally!' he muttered in obvious embarrassment.

'So, Fred!' said Granny. 'What are you two love-birds doing for Valentine's?'

Fred gave a kind of horrid twitch, no doubt at the concept of his being part of a Two Lovebirds Situation, but he managed not to gag by keeping his eyes firmly averted from the vast smelly mountain of cellulite, dandruff and bogies that was his beloved girlfriend Jess.

'There's a – uh, the dinner dance thing,' he growled, as if to show his total indifference to the doomed event.

'Oh, yes, the dinner dance!' cooed Granny happily. 'Grandpa used to take me to dinner dances down at the Royal George Hotel. They had a wonderful buffet there, with seven different kinds of salad!'

'Wow, Granny!' said Jess. 'What sort of dress did you wear?' Anything to divert attention from the subject of catering. Jess was secretly appalled to hear there could be seven different types of salad, and wondered how many types her customers were expecting.

Just as they were finishing dinner, somebody rang the doorbell.

'Get that, would you, Jess, love?' asked Mum.

Jess cringed. 'But, Mum, I look so gross!' She pulled disgustedly at her jog-pants.

'If Fred doesn't mind, why should anybody else?' asked Granny with a naughty wink.

Wearily and apprehensively, Jess dragged herself to the door, pulling down the fleece to try and hide, well, everything. Gingerly, she opened the door. It was Martin.

'Martin!' Jess cheered up. Martin's return was good news: it meant he was still interested in Mum. But he was about to walk into a cosy family dinner with Dad apparently totally back in town. 'Come in!' Jess's mind was like a thunderstorm: black rumbles of dread punctuated by sudden desperate flashing ideas. 'We're just in the middle of Dad's farewell dinner! He's off to Barcelona in the morning to join his boyfriend – you knew he was gay, didn't you?' She was doing her best to reassure him.

Martin nodded slightly awkwardly and stepped inside. 'How's Fred?' he asked, looking down at her with a kindly smile. It was so nice of him to remember Fred's name.

'He's here – you can meet him!' she said. As he took his coat off, Martin looked towards the kitchen with a tiny, thoughtful frown. Jess wondered if he was nervous about Mum and Dad possibly getting back together again. Well, she had done her best, inventing that reunion with Phil in Barcelona.

Chapter 20

'Martin!' cried Dad, getting up with a welcoming kind of wave. Jess glared at Dad. Martin was Mum's friend – Dad should just sit quietly and stop acting as if he was the boss around here. 'You haven't met Fred, have you?' Dad went on.

Martin nodded and grinned, and Fred did one of his self-conscious twitches.

'Hi, Fred!' said Martin. 'I've heard a lot about you. Hello!' Then he smiled at Granny, who greeted him with politeness but not warmth. Oh God! Maybe Granny had got it into her head that Mum and Dad might be heading for a reconciliation, and now viewed Martin as a dangerous threat. 'So, Madeleine,' Martin continued – rather nervously, Jess thought, 'how were things at the library today?'

'Somebody died on us this morning,' said Mum

with a tired shrug. 'Otherwise, fine.'

'You never told me somebody died, Madeleine!' exclaimed Granny resentfully. As the resident murder buff, no doubt she felt unjustly excluded. 'Was it natural causes?'

'No,' said Mum. 'A woman clubbed her husband to death with an encyclopedia.' Mum had a strange demented look, as if she was planning to do something similar before bedtime.

'Oh, Madeleine, you are a one!' Granny sighed, and turned to Martin with a strange, manipulative look in her eye. 'She's always been a terrible fibber ever since she was small. You never know where you are with Madeleine! Somehow Tim's got used to it over the years, though I don't know how he does it – he's a hero.' Oh no! She really was trying to put Martin off Mum!

Jess stared at Granny in disbelief. How many lies could the old girl cram into one brief speech? Mum was so not a fibber – the reference to death by encyclopedia had been an obvious joke. You *always* knew where you were with Mum, and Dad had *never* got used to it over the years – and that phrase suggested he had somehow been present over the years, whereas they'd been lucky to see him every three

157

months or so. Lastly, Dad was about as far from being a hero as it is possible to be.

'Was it one of those street people who died?' asked Dad, gazing at Mum in awe. He would never have the bottle to deal with a dead body. He would run off screaming and lock himself in the bathroom if there was even a dead mouse behind the fridge.

'No, it was a little old lady,' said Mum. 'She fainted in the reference section and she sort of never came round. We placed her in the recovery position but it didn't work.' There was a brief awful depressed kind of pause. Fred was staring fanatically at the table. He was usually so witty; why couldn't he say something funny or helpful, or at least catch Jess's eye in a conspiratorial hysterical stare?

'I always go to bed in the recovery position,' Granny confided to Martin, 'in case I faint in my sleep.'

Martin looked impressed. 'Probably a good idea,' he said. 'I should try it.'

'Would you like a coffee, Martin?' asked Mum at last. She was so clueless, thought Jess. She should offer him some pudding, too. There was an orange cake thing on top of the fridge and Jess's Binge Radar could sense whipped cream in the fridge.

'No, thanks,' said Martin, looking awkward.

'Have some tea, then!' cried Jess, taking the initiative as the grown-ups seemed to be so useless and inhospitable, and Martin still hadn't sat down. 'Or some herbal tea!' Jess rushed to the fridge and carefully picked up the cake. She placed it in the middle of the table.

'Wait until we've cleared the plates, Jess,' said Mum, clattering about busily. 'Do sit down, Martin!' At last! Anybody would think she hated the guy, even though she'd confided to Jess that he was half-gorgeous.

'You missed a great fish pie,' said Dad, slapping his tum in a complacent way. 'Although I say so myself.'

'It's OK,' murmured Martin, sitting down gingerly on the edge of one of the spare chairs – as if he wanted to minimise his presence somehow. 'I've eaten.'

'Ordinary tea or herbal tea, Martin?' asked Jess politely. She was determined to keep him there. He mustn't rush off again. He must understand that he was the one who made Mum happy – not Dad. She cast a desperate look at Fred, hoping in vain for a bit of support. He was examining his fingers. Fred was so

159

hilarious when they were alone, but sometimes, amongst adults, he could kind of switch off and become rather like a subdued ghost. It was only his way of being shy, really, and Jess felt a surge of compassion for him at the same time as wanting to give him a hearty kick in the pants.

'Ordinary tea, please, Jess,' said Martin, still kind of edgy and obviously trying to read the matrimonial situation.

'And you will have a piece of cake?' Mum was becoming a bit more confident and fired up now, bustling about with the dessert plates.

'Well, OK, thanks,' said Martin. 'It looks delicious!' He gave Granny an ingratiating smile.

'It's one of my friend Deborah's cakes,' said Granny. Granny then started rambling on and on about Deborah, including details of her strange rash, which broke out every time she was exposed to lycra – even just watching the Tour de France on TV could make poor Deborah itch. Everybody else sipped their tea and nibbled their cake, praying to be rescued from Granny's droning monologue – a power cut would have been just the ticket. Eventually Granny paused to burp discreetly, and Fred pounced on his opportunity.

'I, er, I ought to go,' he said, scrambling awk-wardly to his feet. Jess jumped up, too. 'Haven't done my homework,' Fred added, putting on an angelic face, even though Jess knew he very rarely did his homework before 11 p.m.

'I'll see you out,' she murmured.

After Fred had managed to say his thank-yous and goodbyes, and had climbed into his parka without knocking any furniture over (a first), they slipped out into the hall.

'Guess what?' hissed Jess happily. 'Dad found the Chaos money! It had slipped down behind my desk! I'm so, so sorry, Fred. I just thought you must have had it because I got confused about the times when you did have it, and I'd looked and looked every-where, and I said all those horrid things to you and I'm really, really sorry.' She threw her arms around him and gave him a massive hug. But she could feel that Fred wasn't responding. She stood back and stared up at him. 'What's the matter?' she asked. He looked sheepish and started kicking invisible things about.

'Yeah, um . . . the reason I called by . . .' he began, and his eyes swivelled uneasily all over the walls, the front door, the doormat, the radiator '. . . is that . . .

uhh, this is really, like, awkward, but, uh . . . Frenzy have let me down.'

'What do you mean?' Jess's heart gave an alarmed lurch. Just when they had found the money and things could be organised properly at last, the band had somehow let Fred down?

'They, uh, they can't do the gig after all,' muttered Fred lamely.

'But they promised!' seethed Jess indignantly. 'You told me they promised you! Who are they, anyway? I'll ring them up right now.'

'You can't do that,' said Fred nervously. 'They've, uh, they've just been offered a recording contract in – in Germany.' Something about Fred's face suddenly rang alarm bells at the back of Jess's mind. She peered suspiciously into his face.

'Fred, are you being straight with me? Is this really, really true? You're lying, aren't you?'

'No, no!' Fred assured her, kicking more imaginary things about. He blushed – always a giveaway.

'Well, give me their number, then, and I'll ring them!' demanded Jess. Fred heaved a huge shuddering sigh. Jess knew what was coming now – the truth. She braced herself.

'The fact is,' said Fred tragically, looking down at the doormat, 'there is no Frenzy.'

'What?' Jess was incredulous.

'I made them up.'

'You did *what*?!?'

'I invented them.'

'Why, in God's name?'

'Because everything was getting so out of hand,' gabbled Fred, waving his hands about. 'You were giving me such a hard time –'

'I was just trying to organise things, Fred. Somebody has to!'

'I know, I know. There *was* a band called Frenzy, and Mackenzie said he knew the drummer's brother, and he said he could get them to come and do the gig, but it turned out they'd disbanded before Christmas. I didn't *totally* invent them.'

'But you told me they could play at the dinner dance!'

'Yes, but it was only to buy a bit of time. I knew you were in a stress – I wanted you to feel that part of it was all fixed up.'

'Oh yeah?' Jess was sceptical about this. 'Or was it just to get me off your back?'

Fred shook his head, said nothing and now stared

tragically at the radiator. 'I will fix something up, I promise,' he said, suddenly looking into her eyes. 'I can't bear letting you down like this. I will find a band somewhere, *really*. Give me time.'

And then he was gone, out into the night.

The next few days passed in a flash. The money was at last safe in the bank, and Jess spent hours in the supermarket writing down the prices of salads and hams and quiches and stuff. But how much of it would you need to feed nearly a hundred people?

By the time Friday came, Jess had entered a trance-like state. With only a week to go before lift-off, Jess just had to believe it could be organised, and that a cold buffet would be OK, even though it was February. She would have to ask Flora to help her work out the portions and the cost and everything. And she'd have to ask Mum to collect it all in her beat-up old estate car, and she'd have to ask some of her friends to help . . . How much help would she need? It was a continuing nightmare.

As for the band situation, Fred simply refused to discuss it. He seemed to spend ages on his mobile talking to people, and he'd dropped some hints that he'd reopened negotiations with Goldilocks. When

Jess asked how it was going, he always said the same old thing: 'Trust me!' The trouble was, Jess didn't trust him. She trusted him as a comedian, but as an events manager? Hardly.

Now the trip to Dorset had stopped seeming like an obstacle, and started to feel like a wonderful escape from a bad dream. In fact, one of Jess's more feverish fantasies involved running off into the Dorset countryside, inventing a new identity as Tess the goatherd, and never going home again.

Chapter 21

'Right,' said Mum, driving them to the station on Friday evening after school. 'Mrs Stevens is going to meet you at Weymouth.'

Jess and Fred, sitting together in the back, taxi style, exchanged an amused look, and Jess rolled her eyes apologetically and squeezed his hand. They were going down to Dorset by train because Jack's car had developed a radiator leak, and there was only enough room in the Stevenses' people carrier for Jack's parents, Jack, Flora, Jack's brother George and his mates from uni.

'Get a seat in the middle carriage of the train!' Mum went on.

'Why?' Jess tried not to get too irritated.

'Because if there's a crash, the front and back carriages usually get the worst of it!' God, Mum was

166

paranoid about crashes.

'I've always loved trains.' Fred tried to turn the conversation in more positive directions. 'Maybe I was a trainspotter in a previous life! I've got vague memories of hanging around stations in my anorak as the Duke of Cumberland went thundering past in a shower of sparks and smoke. I was quite impressed by the trains, too.'

'For God's sake, help with the washing up!' Mum continued her pep talk, ignoring Fred's ravings. 'And don't sit up talking all night when Mr and Mrs Stevens are trying to sleep.'

'As if we would!' sighed Jess, secretly imagining the banshee wail with which she was planning to wake Mr and Mrs Stevens at 3 a.m.

'And make sure you do all the food preparation,' said Mum, peering through the darkness as the station lights loomed up. 'And lay the table! And don't play silly games on the cliffs in the dark. Promise me you won't go near the cliff edge? Fred, promise me you won't let her anywhere near the cliff edge!'

'I promise,' said Fred. 'I won't even let her go anywhere near the food mixer.'

'That would be a worse death, after all,' Jess

pointed out. 'Although some people might say it would be poetic justice for me to end up as a hamburger.' The feeling of going away, even just for the weekend, had filled Jess with a crazy kind of relief and joy.

They climbed out of the car and got their bags out of the boot. Jess's mum stood watching them with a terrible doom-laden frown of anxiety, as if they were setting out for a war zone. She launched herself at Jess and hugged her so hard, there was a faint cracking noise. Jess knew her mum was convinced they would never meet again – in this life, anyway.

'Enjoy your weekend, Mum,' she said, prising Mum's frantic fingers off her arm. 'Are you seeing Martin?'

'Oh, I don't know!' said Mum in an irritable way. 'Never mind about me. You just keep safe, that's all.'

The train was packed, and Jess and Fred had to stand in the area by the buffet.

'I so love trains!' Jess grinned, clutching her lemonade can as the train swayed through the dark. 'I wish we could just stay on this train all night and end up in Moscow or something.'

'We should go on one of those epic train journeys

one day,' suggested Fred. 'You know, across the Great Mongolian Plain or whatever. To China or India or something. Wait! Let's pretend we've never met before. I'll go to the loo and when I come out, we'll be strangers on the Vladivostok Express.'

Jess leaned on the counter with the bored look of a heroine in one of those moody black-and-white 1940s films. Fred emerged from the loo with his collar turned up – the idiot. Jess ignored him. He trod heavily on her toe.

'Oh, excuse me!' he said, in a deep Russian sort of voice. 'I'm so sorry. The train lurches so badly whenever we hit a peasant. Is your foot badly hurt?'

'It's all right,' Jess assured him in a snaky, husky hiss. 'My right foot is made of iron. I lost it in the uprising in Omsk.'

'Were you shot by the Bolsheviks?' Fred loved history, but Jess couldn't remember who the Bolsheviks were.

'No,' she informed him. 'It was a very uncomfortable pair of shoes. I was at a ball with Prince Obergurgle – we danced all night and in the morning my foot fell off. So what? I never liked it anyway.' She shrugged.

'Not the same Prince Obergurgle who was shot by

the Bolsheviks?' asked Fred, looking impressed.

'It may have been.' Jess gave another charismatic shrug. 'Who cares? My next lover was a plough-boy. He was a lot more fun than the prince.'

'You are a very attractive person, if I may say so,' hissed Fred in her ear. 'Can I offer you a job in my spy network?'

'I'm already a double agent,' Jess replied snootily. 'But I might be able to fit you in on Thursday afternoons.'

Fred laughed. Then his face changed; the Russian spy expression fell away and he was Fred again.

'We could always just cancel it,' he said, suddenly deadly serious. Jess's heart gave a horrid skip. 'We could say it's due to unforeseen circumstances,' Fred went on. 'People cancel things all the time. We've banked the money now so we could give everybody a refund.'

'But people would think we were such losers!' cried Jess. 'And they'd be right! And what about Oxfam? We can't let them down!'

Fred shook his head. 'Everybody will have forgotten all about it by Easter.'

'I don't know . . .' Jess hesitated. 'I can't face the idea of cancelling it – not at the moment, anyway.

There must be a way to get the food and music organised properly!'

'Hmmm,' Fred said doubtfully, and shrugged.

'Fred, let's talk about this later,' suggested Jess. 'I just want to relax and enjoy myself this evening, OK? We'll talk about it in the morning. Let's get back to the Vladivostok Express.'

But somehow the mood had changed and the world of Russian spies had evaporated.

When they arrived at Weymouth it did seem as dark and foggy as Outer Mongolia, but through a freezing mist Jess spotted Flora waiting on the platform, huddled deep in her parka, her breath billowing on the cold night air.

'God, it's amazing!' Flora hugged her as if they'd been parted for years, not hours. 'Wait till you see the house! It's such a shame it's dark but apparently in the morning we're gonna be blown away by the view! Jack's mum is parked outside . . . Her scent is Winter Spice, by the way.'

'My scent is damp dog,' murmured Fred.

Jess punched him affectionately.

'Gubbins is so wonderful! We took him down to the beach in the dark and he was frightened of the sea! He was barking at the waves, trying to frighten them! God, it was hilarious!'

Waiting in the people carrier, Mrs Stevens was wreathed in a cashmere throw and a delicious cloud of Winter Spice. She flashed them a toothy grin.

'Hello, how lovely to meet you, Fred. And, Jess, you're looking wonderful, how was your journey?' she gushed in her breathy voice.

'Fine, thanks,' said Jess politely. 'How was yours?' (She was particularly proud of this bit of ultra-politeness, and would remember to boast about it to Mum when she got back.)

'Oh, it was fine, thank you, Jess, but the roads are always a bit busy on Friday evenings, aren't they? Even in winter. I hope Charles has got the house warmed up – the boys have been cutting wood. We've got a big fireplace so you'll be able to toast your bottoms all evening.'

Mrs Stevens drove out of town with panache; soon they were on dark country roads.

'I wish we could see the sea!' sighed Jess.

'Oh, you wait till tomorrow morning – you won't be disappointed, unless there's fog,' promised Mrs Stevens.

Eventually they turned off the country road into a small lane and then almost immediately up a zigzagging steep sandy drive, higher and higher and higher, until Jess's ears popped. A big house loomed up in the headlamps, and Mrs Stevens parked.

'Welcome to Sea Spray,' she beamed, tossing her blonde hair back with the kind of relaxed poise that Jess's mother would never have managed in a million years. 'We've saved some supper for you – you must be starving!'

'Oh, thanks very much!' Jess replied eagerly.

They entered the house via the kitchen, which was at the back, and then went through into a huge sitting room where a gang of boys were gathered around a fireplace. A bald man, presumably Mr Stevens, was dozing in an armchair. Jack jumped to his feet as they arrived and came over, smiling, the puppy bounding alongside him.

'Hi, Jess! Hi, Fred!' he said. 'How was the train? We got the fire going for you. Uh, I don't think you know my bro George . . .' A smaller and slightly plumper version of Jack waved from the hearthrug. He looked a bit like a Roman emperor with dark curly hair and a big nose. 'And this is Tom and Humph.' Tom was tall with glasses and a smile a mile wide, and Humph was a pale, thin guy kneeling by the fire and fiddling with a poker.

173

'There are so many boys, we could almost have a football match!' trilled Mrs Stevens from the kitchen. 'We've saved some chicken casserole and some spuds in their jackets for you, if that's OK, Jess?'

'Oh wonderful, thanks so much!' Jess turned back to the kitchen and Fred followed her.

Gubbins was wagging and capering round their feet – he seemed to be particularly enchanted by Jess, and the feeling was mutual. She'd always wanted a dog and had nagged her mum about it in vain for years.

There was a big table in the kitchen with two places set for them.

'Sit down!' said Flora. 'What would you like to drink? OJ or cranberry?'

'Just water, please.' Jess was uneasily aware that her jeans were already too tight, and she hadn't hit the spuds yet.

'So,' said Mrs Stevens, 'when you've had your supper, we'll all gather round the fire and play charades until we fall asleep. It's a tradition at Sea Spray.'

'Charades?' Jess clapped her hands. 'We love charades, don't we, Fred?'

'I'm not sure I'll be able to play,' said Fred. 'I've strained my imagination.'

Mrs Stevens looked baffled for a moment, and then uttered a strange bellowing laugh. 'Oh, Fred!' she cried. 'Flora warned me that you were a bit of a joker! Strained your imagination! Ha, ha!'

Jess was glad that Mrs Stevens had apparently found Fred amusing, but she knew his manner could be a bit weird sometimes, and she just hoped he would relax and not try too hard.

Chapter 22

After gobbling up the delicious supper, expressing delight and gratitude and insisting on washing up their plates (winning a gold star for politeness – Mum would be proud), Jess and Fred returned to the sitting room. Mr Stevens was still asleep in his chair, Gubbins was curled up on the sofa with Flora, and Jack, George, Tom and Humph were sprawled on the floor, arguing. There were loads of chairs and three sofas – the room was enormous – so Fred and Jess sat down, slightly awkwardly, on a small sofa.

'But I've gotta find that phone!' Humph was saying, running his fingers through his limp fair hair and turning his big green panicky eyes from person to person.

'Humph lost his mobile earlier this evening,' Jack explained with an amused grin. 'We went out to walk on the beach and he reckons he must have dropped it somewhere on the path.'

'What if it rains?' wailed Humph. He seemed to be a bit of a drama queen.

'Oh, you can just put it in the microwave to dry it out,' said Jack, exchanging a quick flickering secret smile with his brother George.

'Can you?' Humph looked doubtful. 'That sounds a bit, uh, dodgy!'

'No, it's fine!' said George. He had a lazy kind of grin. He lay back and stared at the ceiling, scratching his face. 'We could put the dog in, too, if he gets a bit wet in the sea.'

'Nooooo!' shrieked Flora, laughing. 'Don't you dare touch my precious Gubbins!'

'A girl said that to me once at a party,' said George mischievously, 'but I was too drunk to listen and got beaten up by her boyfriend.'

Mrs Stevens appeared in the doorway, her hands covered with flour. She'd already confessed to being an obsessive about baking – always a welcome hobby in a parent. 'Why don't you all play charades?' she suggested. 'Round the fire – so cosy!'

'Later, Mum.' George brushed her suggestion aside.

'I'd love to play charades,' said Jess, knowing it was something she and Fred would really enjoy. Fred was brilliant at charades. She'd never forget his performance of *Mamma Mia!* – the whole concept.

'So would I!' added Flora. 'Although I'm rubbish at it!'

'Let's go down to the beach again first!' suggested Jack. He gave Flora a secret kind of look, and Jess noticed George picking up on it. She guessed something was brewing.

Tom, the quiet speccy guy with the big smile, lumbered to his feet. 'Maybe we'll find Humph's phone,' he said, and Jess saw that he, too, was in on the joke – whatever it was.

'Yeah!' George got up. 'Hey, mate! We could ring your phone as we go down the path and we might hear its ringtone!'

'My phone's dead though!' fretted Humph. 'I left my charger behind! Maybe I should hitch into Weymouth tomorrow and get a new charger, except I'm right out of cash. Could you lend me ten quid, George?'

'I'd really love to go down to the beach, wouldn't you, Fred?' Jess jumped up and ran to get her coat.

'Take care on that path,' warned Mrs Stevens.

'Oh, I promised my mum I'd plummet to my doom at the earliest opportunity!' Jess assured her. 'So don't worry – no, I mean, *really* don't worry. I'm the most careful person in the universe!'

'There are loads of wellies outside on the veranda,' said Mrs Stevens. 'There's bound to be a pair your size. Much better for wet sand.'

'Yes, put your wellies on, everyone!' called George, as they filed out of a front door on to a covered veranda. Jess could hear the sound of the sea down below. 'Here are yours, Tom,' said George, fussing over a row of wellies. He seemed to be something of a control freak. 'Tom Barker, size twelve, the mind of a pygmy inside a giant's body. Here are yours, bruv.' He tossed a pair to Jack, who sniggered in a mysterious way. 'And here are yours, Humph!' George handed a pair to Humph, who had got the zip to his anorak stuck – he seemed to be a disorganised scatterbrain.

'Cheers,' said Humph. He abandoned his struggle with the zip, grabbed the wellies and started to wriggle into them. 'Wait!' he said, puzzled and hopping about. 'There's something – something inside my welly . . .' He pulled his foot out, peered inside the welly by the light of the porch and recoiled with a yell of disgust. 'Ugh! Dog shit!! Guys, that is disgusting! Jesus! That stinks!'

'God, we really have to train Gubbins,' giggled Jack. 'He keeps crapping in the wellies. Sorry, mate!'

The boys all cracked up. George sank down on to a bench nearby, laughing helplessly, while poor Humph hopped about, wailing.

'It's all over my sock! God, it's revolting! I'll have to take my sock off, but I haven't brought a spare pair. Can you lend me a spare sock, George, you sadist?'

But George couldn't speak – he was still helpless and shaking. Jess smiled politely at the trick, though it wasn't her sort of humour. This was evidently the way these guys passed their time. It was like that American TV stunt programme *Jackass*. Jess stole a sidelong glance at Fred. He was watching with a wry smile, but he looked kind of vulnerable. Fred's weapon was his deadly wit. He wasn't really comfortable with rugger-jock horseplay.

They started down the cliff path. George led the way, shining a torch behind him, a bit like an usher in a cinema. Humph was wearing a different pair of wellies and only one sock, and he never stopped talking, alternately moaning about his naked foot and lamenting his lost phone.

'I'm sure we'll find it in the morning, as soon as it gets light.' Flora was trying to comfort him.

'Yeah, but somebody could steal it!' complained Humph in his high-pitched whining voice. 'Or maybe a seagull will nick it or something.'

'Seagulls don't nick metal objects,' said tall smiley Tom. 'Not like magpies. It's your pasties you want to worry about.'

'Yeah!' sniggered George. 'Hold on to your pasties, guys!'

The path, though tricky and steep, never felt very dangerous because on the seaward side there was a kind of low wall of turf.

'Thank God for Dad's alcohol ban!' said George. 'If I was pissed I'd be headfirst over here and rolling right down to the rocks!'

Eventually they reached the beach – without finding Humph's phone – and ran about screaming as people do who find themselves by the sea on a winter night. The waves crashed, black and white and mighty, so close they could feel the spray.

'If it was summer we could have a swim,' said George, 'but frankly, right now, I'd just as soon not freeze my pasties off!'

Flora and Jess stared at the sea in a trance of delight, huddled together arm in arm, while the guys ran up and down kicking sand about. At one stage they picked Humph up and ran towards the sea with him, pretending they were about to throw him in, changing direction at the last minute and throwing him back up the beach instead.

'God!' exclaimed Jess. 'I feel quite sorry for Humph!'

'Oh, no need to,' Flora reassured her. 'They always seem to behave like this, and I think he likes it.'

Fred was hovering nearby, his collar turned up against the cold wind.

'Why don't you go and horse around with the guys, Fred?' asked Jess uneasily.

'I'd rather be an honorary member of the girls' club just right now, if you don't mind,' murmured Fred. 'I'm such a weakling, if they tried to throw me in the sea I'd probably break a leg.'

'Isn't it absolutely awesome here!' sighed Jess, staring up at the stars as the surf crashed nearby. 'God, Flo, it's really, really kind of them to invite me and Fred!'

'Oh, no problem,' said Flora with a happy smile.

'Mrs Stevens really loves entertaining, and I'm always talking about you two guys. And besides . . . I think you can both do with a break from all that stressy Chaos stuff.'

'Oh, don't mention that!' Jess shuddered. 'I wanted to forget about it just for one night. Tomorrow we have to come up with a plan, Fred!'

'But do we?' Fred shrugged. 'It's not the only solution.'

'Fred was saying, on the train,' Jess explained, 'that he thinks we should just cancel the whole thing and give people their money back.'

Flora hesitated. 'I wouldn't rule it out, babe,' she said uncertainly. 'It wouldn't be the end of the world. Things get cancelled all the time.'

'That's just what I said,' put in Fred swiftly.

'But it would be so awful!' wailed Jess. 'Just to give up! I hate giving up! People would think we were so lame – and they'd be right.'

'No, they wouldn't,' said Flora. 'They'd understand.'

'But they'd be so disappointed!' Jess argued. 'They're looking forward to it! And they're trusting us to organise it!'

'But the stress of it is driving you round the

bend, Jess,' Flora insisted gently. 'You said so yourself this morning. If you decided to cancel it – decided here and now – you could just relax and enjoy the weekend. It would be such a load off your mind.'

Jess was silent for a moment. The idea of cancelling Chaos did seem wonderfully attractive. No food to organise, no music to fix up, no more terror and dread, just lovely, lovely nothing to worry about except writing out a few cheques as refunds. Jess trembled – she was so very, very tempted.

'I'll think it over,' she conceded. 'But I don't want to talk about it any more this evening, OK?'

Fred and Flora exchanged a dubious glance, and nodded. Flora threw her arm round Jess. 'Don't forget, babe,' she said finally, 'there's no need to be a hero.'

At this moment the guys ran past, holding Humph on their shoulders like a rocket launcher. They were whooping and poor Humph was screaming.

'Oh God,' muttered Fred. 'Manly games. I should be bonding with them but somehow I'd rather eat a live horse.'

'Well, you've got to share the dorm with them tonight,' said Flora ominously, 'so maybe you should look really, really carefully into your bed before you get into it.'

'Will do!' Fred nodded. He did look a teeny bit worried.

Chapter 23

'Jess, wake up and look at this amazing view!' Flora's face appeared in a hole in Jess's dream. 'Come on! You can see the sea! You can see right along the coast to Weymouth!'

Jess yawned and stretched and crawled out of bed.

'Put your jumper on!' Flora went on. 'Come out on to the veranda!' She was wearing her parka.

Their little bedroom was on the ground floor but round at the side of the house – the only view from their window was of a kind of lean-to where all the logs were stored. But once Jess had scrambled into her clothes, they went into the sitting room, through the French windows and on to the veranda. The view there was just awesome: the house, perched apparently alone on its cliff, seemed surrounded by sea far below. The coastline curved round in the furthest distance, like a thin grey line drawn in pencil, where there was the hint of tiny distant rooftops and the outlines of buildings.

'That's Weymouth!' breathed Flora in admiration. 'Oh, isn't it wonderful! I'm so glad the sun is shining. The sea looks so blue.'

'But it's kind of gold, too,' sighed Jess. The ocean seemed ultra-calm, stretching away in glassy glowing sheets towards the distant horizon, colours moving across it as clouds drifted over the sun. 'Fred's got to see this!' She turned and went back into the living room.

There was the hubbub of boys' voices from the kitchen, and they found the guys sitting at the huge kitchen table, eating their breakfast: Jack and George tucking into bacon and eggs, Tom shovelling muesli into his enormous mouth, and Humph fiddling with a boiled egg and cursing as the yolk ran over his fingers. But no Fred.

'Help yourselves to breakfast, ladies!' grinned George, presiding over the breakfast table like a Roman emperor. 'The Parents usually have a lie-in to avoid the revolting sight of us eating.'

'Where's Fred?' asked Jess. A naughty glinting smile flashed around the gang of boys. Something had happened. Jess's heart gave a sickening lurch.

'Oh, he's having a lie-in, too,' said George. 'Poor Fredianus! I don't think he slept very well.'

'You didn't play any horrible tricks on him, did you, guys?' demanded Flora.

Jack and George put on a stagy show of innocence.

'What, us?' asked George. 'We're just pussy cats! Pass the marmalade, Humph, you useless parasite!'

It was obvious there was some joke going on, but the boys' gang was kind of buttoned-down and pretending nothing was the matter. Jess didn't want to get all stressy, even though she felt alarmed and anxious.

'What shall we have for breakfast, Jess?' Flora looked sympathetic but embarrassed; she knew Jess would be worried about Fred, but as a guest in her boyfriend's house she was clearly trying to behave perfectly to everybody in all directions. 'How about some scrambled eggs?' she went on. 'With tomatoes and mushrooms? That's your favourite, isn't it?'

'Yeah,' said Jess. 'Shall I do the mushrooms and tomatoes while you do the scrambling? You're the Demon Scrambler.'

As she wiped and sliced the mushrooms, Jess tried

not to worry. So Fred was having a lie-in. So what? He often slept till noon at weekends; his mum was always joking about it. There was no need to worry. She tried not to listen to the boys' conversation, and to concentrate on what Flora was saying about the lovely walks they could have along the cliffs and down on the beach, but it was hard to get George's buzzing voice out of her head.

'Guys! You know Mum likes charades? Well, we could arrange a little scene to greet her when she comes into the kitchen . . . a massacre! Humph slumped over his plate with ketchup coming out of his ear, Tom lying on the floor with a dot of ketchup in the middle of his forehead, and you impaled on the breadboard, bruv, with the bread knife sticking out of your back.'

'Waste of ketchup,' said Jack, licking his fingers. 'Plus I don't like the sound of that bread knife bit.'

'We could get one of those trick knives from the joke shop in Weymouth,' said George. He seemed to be the gang leader. He never stopped talking. Jess had heard of something called 'small man syndrome' – apparently Napoleon was a bit of a hobbit, and there's this theory that men who aren't very tall can burn up loads of energy trying to prove that, though short, when it comes to achievements they are the biggest of big shots.

'I wouldn't mind going into Weymouth,' said Humph. 'I need to get a charger – can anyone lend me ten quid?'

'Shouldn't you find your phone first?' asked big Tom patiently as if Humph was a child. 'What's the point of a charger if you haven't got a phone?'

'I found Humph's phone this morning when I went down for my jog on the beach,' said George, slapping his head as if he'd just remembered. There was something stagy about the way he did it. 'I dried it off in the microwave for you, buddy. It's still there.'

'What?' Humph jumped to his feet, his green eyes wild with excitement. He raced to the microwave, threw open the door and took out a mobile. He examined it and stared accusingly at George. Jess watched, fascinated but fearful. 'You didn't really dry it off in here, did you?' Humph asked, puzzled.

'Sure!' said George, his eyes dancing. 'Give it another blast if you don't believe me. Half a minute at maximum should do the trick.'

Humph stood, hesitating and frowning, glancing at his phone and then at the microwave. Then he reached for the door.

'Don't!' yelled Jess. She couldn't help herself. 'It'll explode!'

Humph stared at her and the other boys groaned.

'It's metal!' said Jess.

Humph turned to George. 'You didn't!' he said with a slinky grin. 'You've been ripping the piss out of me! I'll get you for this, George Stevens!' But he seemed strangely pleased to have been the victim of another trick. 'Did you really find it on the path? Where?'

'George picked your phone up off the table yesterday afternoon,' explained speccy Tom admiringly. 'You never know where it is anyway. George reckoned he could make you cook it this morning.' Jess was revising her opinion of big speccy Tom. At first she'd thought he was the gentlest of the guys but he seemed to hero-worship George. 'You owe me five quid, mate,' Tom went on. 'I told you he'd never fall for it.'

'He would have!' protested George. 'If Little Miss Head Prefect here hadn't butted in.'

Jess felt a flare of furious indignation. 'You could have ruined Humph's phone,' she pointed out, sounding indeed rather Head Prefectish – a horrible feeling for Jess, like the way she'd felt when Fred couldn't be serious about organising Chaos. Jess hated being teacherish – she was usually a bit of a rebel.

'My phone's rubbish anyway,' said Humph, refusing her support and siding with the boys who had played the trick on him. 'Maybe I could have claimed back the insurance and bought a better one. Hey! Let's do it, guys.'

The boys then settled into an argument about what would happen if you put a mobile phone into a microwave, while Jess and Flora ate their breakfast in silence. There was a slightly weird atmosphere. Jess didn't have much of an appetite and Flora's scrambled eggs lacked their usual divine fluffiness and were kind of stringy. Where was Fred? Jess couldn't think about anything else, although every other moment she felt she was being over-anxious and stupid. What could be more normal than a lie-in?

Shortly afterwards, while Jess and Flora were washing up, Mrs Stevens entered in a beige woolly dressing gown, accompanied by Gubbins.

'The view!' she raved. 'Isn't it heavenly! Charles said it was going to rain today – he's useless. Have you all had breakfast? Where's Fred?'

There was a moment's naughty pause again. You could feel the electricity in the air. The guys' faces were full of flickering mischief.

'He's having a lie-in, poor old Fredianus,' said George. 'He couldn't sleep all night because of O'Connell snoring.'

'I don't snore!' retorted speccy Tom. 'If Fred couldn't sleep it wasn't because of me.'

'Couldn't Fred sleep?' asked Jess anxiously.

'Well, I reckon he's asleep now,' said George with a devilish grin. 'Listen!' He held up a finger. There was silence. 'Hear anything? No! No distant cries for help. Only the sound . . . of silence.' For a split second Jess had a horrible sort of hallucination that George had killed Fred, that George was some kind of crazed serial murderer and later that day he was going to kill them all, one by one, in a mad game of charades.

'Is it OK if I go and wake him up?' she said, suddenly determined to do something – anything – to make sure Fred was OK.

'Yes, of course, Jess,' smiled Mrs Stevens. 'Tell him I'll put some toast on.'

'There goes the Head Prefect,' said George with a titter, as Jess headed for the stairs. 'Poor old Fred!'

Jess gritted her teeth. She was trying not to hate George, but it was a challenge.

The stairs were the kind of open-tread wooden sort you get in old barns, and they led directly up into a huge attic which ran the whole length of the house. There were about eight single beds in there, arranged in two rows just like a school dormitory. And every bed was empty. Fred was nowhere to be seen. Jess stared in disbelief. There were five messy beds, where the boys had evidently slept, strewn with the boy debris of smelly socks and stuff, and three untouched beds. Jess's heart was hammering away like mad. Where was Fred?

At the far end of the room she noticed a closed door. She tiptoed down to it. There was a sign hanging on it which read: *THIS IS IT!* Presumably it was a bathroom or loo. Jess hesitated by the door.

'Fred!' she called softly.

'Unlock the door,' came Fred's voice immediately, from behind the blue painted boards. Jess noticed that there was a bolt on her side of the door which was drawn across. Hastily she unbolted it and opened the door. Fred walked out, still in his pyjamas and shivering.

'They locked you in!' Jess gasped, clapping her hand across her mouth. 'But you must have been in there for . . .'

'Two hours,' Fred said quietly, but with a heavy dash of venom.

'Two hours!' whispered Jess in disbelief. 'They told me you were having a lie-in!'

'There's no need to go mental about it,' said Fred stiffly. 'Go back down. I'll get dressed and be there in a minute.'

'Why didn't you shout?'

'I wouldn't give them the satisfaction,' said Fred grimly.

'Mrs Stevens said she's making some toast,' said Jess limply, trying to cheer him up.

'Toast!' Fred gave a quiet, bitter laugh. 'As far as these guys are concerned, I *am* toast.'

Jess headed for the stairs, her mind reeling. When did a practical joke go too far? Two hours, locked in the freezing loo! Poor Fred! But the essential thing was not to show them it mattered. They must pretend they didn't mind a bit. Or was that spineless? Jess had never felt so confused.

Chapter 24

As Jess re-entered the kitchen, everybody looked at her and there was a kind of horrible expectant pause – the guys all had mischievous grins, and Flora looked nervous.

'He's fine.' Jess forced herself to smile, even though she felt more like shouting. 'Just got detained in the bathroom.'

'Oh no!' Mrs Stevens glared at George, but not sternly – there was a playful look on her face. 'You didn't? George, you are hopeless. I'm so sorry, Jess – it's a stupid tradition here at Sea Spray. Anyone sleeping in the dorm for the first time gets locked in the bathroom. But usually they start to yell the place down and get let out right away.'

'I think Fred was reading or something,' said Jess lightly. 'Why is there a bolt on the outside of the door, by the way?' She tried to sound polite, even though right now she thought that the bolt was the stupidest thing she'd ever seen.

'Well, when it's blowing a gale, that door rattles like crazy and nobody can sleep a wink,' explained Mrs Stevens. 'So we had that bolt installed and it holds the door snugly in place. We never dreamt these wretched boys would use it as a way of tormenting their guests. Oh, hello, Fred! I'm so sorry about my idiotic sons. Let me soothe you with some French toast.'

'Oh, it's fine,' said Fred, putting on his faux grin. 'I've always wanted that kind of peace and quiet. I was really irritated when Jess came and forced me out. I could spend all weekend in there.'

'I wouldn't say that!' warned Humph slyly. 'Or maybe your wish will come true!'

The guys all laughed, and Fred sat down carefully at the table, still wearing the smile he used when he was really, really embarrassed and uncomfortable. Jess longed to give him a massive hug. This was ridiculous. She could feel tears gathering behind her eyes, but the boys mustn't see or she'd never hear the end of it.

'I want to look at that view again,' she said quickly.

'Come on, Flora!' She grabbed her fleece and rushed out. The sea now had a glassy grey look, clouds had covered the sun and a bitter wind was blowing the coarse grass around at their feet.

'Jack's mum said she thinks it might snow,' said Flora, snuggling into her parka. 'Wouldn't that be amazing! I've never seen it snowing on the sea! We could get snowed in and not be able to go back to school!'

Normally Jess would have jumped eagerly into this fun fantasy but she was still seething. 'Can't you stop Jack behaving like an idiot?' she hissed.

Flora looked startled. She blushed. 'What do you mean?' she faltered, biting her lip uneasily.

'You know! Him and his brother! All these stupid jokes! Humiliating poor Fred! And calling me Head Prefect and stuff! And calling Fred Fredianus!'

Flora kind of cringed. 'It's just guys having a laugh!' she said lightly. 'And anyway, Fred was the one who found that name in the first place. What's the problem?'

'It's really stupid and hostile.'

'You're overreacting, Jess.' Flora kept her voice low, and she was trying to sympathise, but she clearly wasn't about to diss her boyfriend and his family, who

198

owned this glorious place. 'Just lighten up,' she went on. 'I mean, they play tricks on Humph all the time and he just laughs it off.'

'Yeah, but Humph is George's friend from uni,' argued Jess. 'He's used to it and stuff. It's part of their routine, you know. Fred's a total stranger – and he's three years younger than them.'

'Are you saying Fred can't take care of himself?' Flora frowned in a disbelieving kind of way. 'Honestly, Jess, he looked fine. I think you should just relax and stop worrying about him. What guy wants to have his girlfriend fussing over him all the time in front of other guys? Just leave him to fight his own battles. I mean, Fred's got a really, really devastating wit. If anybody can fight his corner, he can.'

Jess was silent. Everything Flora had said made perfect sense. She didn't want to spoil this weekend by being stressy and awkward.

'OK,' she said in a low voice. 'I just wish . . .' She paused.

'Wish what?'

'I wish . . . I don't know.' Jess's wish hung in the air, changing shape all the time. What was it, this wish that would change the weekend from an ordeal into a treat? 'Oh, nothing.' Jess had a feeling that if she worked out exactly what she was feeling, it would be the kind of stuff that would upset Flora.

'Let's go in,' she said. They turned from the tremendous view and, as she did so, Jess realised she'd hardly even glanced at it; she'd only seen the rough grass at their feet, whipped by the winter wind.

Indoors, George was lying on his back on one of the sofas and Gubbins was standing on his tummy, licking his face. George was giggling uncontrollably. With his high-pitched voice, he sounded like a harmless little boy. Jess felt ashamed, as if she'd made a fuss about nothing.

'Don't let Gubbins stand on top of you like that!' called Mrs Stevens from the kitchen door. 'He'll think he's dominant over you.' She turned to Jess and Flora. 'We're trying to teach Gubbins that his place is at the bottom of the pack,' she explained. 'Apparently you must never lie on your back and let them sit on your tummy, like George is doing now – push him off, George! – because what George is doing is submissive and it makes Gubbins feel like top dog.'

'We had the same problem with our labrador when she was young,' said Flora. 'My dad had to be ever so firm with her. He wouldn't let her on the sofa or upstairs, and she had to wait behind us when we went through a doorway. And she had to wait for her food until after we had eaten.'

'Labradors are such lovely dogs!' gushed Mrs Stevens. 'This little rascal is a different kettle of fish – aren't you, Trouble?' She swept Gubbins off the sofa and gave him an adoring, exasperated look.

'Who's top dog here, then?' asked Jess, grateful for something else to talk about. Although . . . was it really something else? Or all part of the same problem?

'I'm top dog,' said Mrs Stevens firmly. 'But don't tell Charles I said so!' The idea of telling Mr Stevens anything was a bit far-fetched. So far this weekend, he had been fast asleep and apparently still was. He had woken up the previous evening in his armchair, hauled himself to his feet, nodded to the gang of his children and their friends without wanting to be introduced, said, 'What-ho! I'm for a proper sleep!' and disappeared.

'Mum,' said George, getting up, 'can I take the car into Weymouth? Humph wants to buy a charger and we thought we might mess around there for a couple of hours – get out of your hair.'

'I suppose so,' said Mrs Stevens cautiously. 'Just be careful, OK?'

'Yeah, well, I am insured to drive it and everything,' argued George self-importantly.

'Yes, and don't we know it,' observed his mother with a stern look. 'It cost an absolute fortune to add you to the insurance. Promise you won't start showing off.'

'Would I ever?' George cocked his head playfully – he could have won the Nobel Prize for Showing Off.

Jess felt a horrid cold chill seize her insides. Maybe George would crash the car and they'd all be killed. Although she despised her mum's nervousness around transport, she sometimes felt she'd inherited it. Maybe she and Fred could stay here at the house. But Flora would want them to go into Weymouth with the gang – she would want to be with Jack, and Jack would obviously want to be . . . Oh God, it made Jess feel ratty and giddy.

Fred ventured into the sitting room, looking pale and insecure. Jess was irritated all over again. Why couldn't he stand up for himself and look relaxed?

'Fred!' cried George. 'Sorry we locked you in the bathroom. You came through it with flying colours, though. No one's ever stayed in that long before. How did you do it?'

'I love it in there,' said Fred in an offhand way,

with a faint smile. Jess was encouraged. She was proud of him. 'Hey!' Fred exclaimed. 'What a view!'

'Oh, of course, you haven't seen it yet!' exclaimed Mrs Stevens. 'We've only got those skylights up in the attic. Take Fred out on to the veranda, Jess, and show him the view.'

As it was obvious Fred was perfectly capable of going out and looking at the view without any help, Jess instantly realised that Mrs Stevens wanted to get them out of the way for a moment while she read the riot act to her unruly gang of boys. It was kind of her, but somehow humiliating. Jess hastily made for the French windows.

Out on the veranda, Jess suddenly felt close to tears. Ridiculous! Probably PMT.

'If only . . .' That If Only stuff had come back, and she realised now what it was she was wishing, and now she could say it. '. . . If only we were here on our own!' she sighed. Fred didn't look at her, he just went on staring out to sea.

'What a terrifying thought,' he said. 'The stuff of nightmares.'

This was, of course, just Fred being himself. He always said the opposite of what he was really feeling, especially when it came to personal stuff. '*I've fallen head over heels in hate with you!*' he'd whispered once. It was just his way, and normally Jess loved it, and loved giving as good as she got. They were famous throughout the school for their banter.

'Don't say things like that!' she heard herself plead in a tearful voice.

'For God's sake, don't cry!' muttered Fred, without looking at her. 'Turn the goddam waterworks off or I may just have to vomit!'

'Fred! Don't be so horrible!'

'I'm going back in,' Fred said grumpily, and turned on his heel.

'Well, I'm going for a walk!' snapped Jess. 'And I hope when I come back you'll have worked out how to behave – not just to me, but to these people who've invited us to this amazing place! This should be the best weekend ever!'

Fred paused for a second and glanced back at her. The look in his eye was not friendly. 'Sometimes you do sound just like a head prefect,' he said, and went back indoors.

Chapter 25

Jess stumbled down the cliff path, tears running down her cheeks. How could Fred be so horrible? She was on his side – it must feel awful being picked on by George and Co. They were bullies. Poor Fred! But Fred didn't seem to want her sympathy – or even her company. How had things gone so terribly wrong?

When she reached the beach she just stood there, watching the waves crashing. The freezing wind tugged her hair about and dried her tears. She took a deep breath. She had to stop crying – this was silly. Then, from high above, she heard somebody call her name.

Flora was up by the house, waving. 'Jess! Come on! We're going into Weymouth!'

Jess waved back and did a kind of mad dance to

look as if she had just come down to the beach for a spot of fresh air, not to sulk or have a cry. She climbed back up the path, puffing and panting. Flora was waiting for her at the top, standing on the veranda, snuggled into her parka. She looked puzzled.

'What's going on?' she whispered. 'Have you and Fred had a row?'

'Why?' asked Jess quickly. 'What's he said?'

'Nothing. It was just the way he looked . . . kind of –' Flora stopped because the guys were all bundling out on to the veranda.

'Come on, girls!' yelled George, waving the car keys. 'Weymouth is calling!'

They all trooped around the house to where the people carrier was parked. Fred kept slightly apart, his hood pulled up, kind of hiding in his clothes. Jess ignored him. She sat next to Flora, Fred went and sat in the back next to Tom. Jess wondered if anybody apart from Flora realised what was happening between her and Fred. But then, what *was* happening? It was all so puzzling – and painful.

There was a very strong smell of the Winter Spice scent Mrs Stevens had been wearing yesterday.

'Wow, Jack!' Jess thought she had better try and

make conversation. 'That perfume of your mum's is amazing!'

'Actually, it's Fred's,' said Jack, with a naughty smile.

'My coat's drenched in it,' said Fred in an expressionless voice. 'Somehow, mysteriously, I now smell so divine, the inhabitants of Weymouth will be asked to stay indoors for their own safety.'

Oh no! The boys had sprayed Fred's coat with Mrs Stevens's scent! The guys all laughed, and Jess managed a tight little smile. At least Fred had made a joke of it. He seemed to be getting on better with the guys. But he was ignoring her.

George drove gently down the zigzag approach to Sea Spray, but once they were on the regular roads he accelerated, hurling the car round bends.

'Slow down, bruv!' said Jack uneasily. 'No need to kill us all!'

'God! You're such a wuss!' sneered George, whizzing round another bend and passing a truck by a hair's breadth.

Jess was terrified and her mum's dreadful warnings rang in her ears – though she and Flo were best friends, she had no wish to share a funeral with her. However, the mad thought did whizz through her brain that if she and Fred were killed in a car crash,

Chaos would have to be cancelled.

'Slow down!' she yelled, suddenly furious. 'If you don't, I'll be sick!'

'OK, steady on, Your Maj – you should have said.' George laughed, but he did slow down.

'I get carsick if people drive fast,' insisted Jess, fuming. It was a lie, of course, but Flora secretly squeezed Jess's hand in feverish support and gratitude.

Eventually, at a slower pace, they arrived in Weymouth, parked the car and tumbled out.

Now, thought Jess, *I've got to make sure I get some time on my own with Fred, but without seeming clingy or desperate.*

'I've gotta find a mobile shop!' said Humph.

'I'll come, too,' said George. 'I want to get a look at their new stuff.'

'I'm going to find an internet cafe,' said Tom.

'There's one up in that direction.' George pointed across the long, curving line of shops facing the sea.

'Look!' cried Flora. 'A lingerie boutique! Let's go and take a peek, Jess!'

'You'd better go too, Fredianus,' said George teasingly. 'You look like a lingerie fan on the quiet.' The guys sniggered again.

Fred backed away, wearing his faux smile. 'No, no,' he said. 'I've got stuff to do – I need the internet cafe, too.'

They all agreed to meet in an hour's time at a nearby cafe, and then Flora dragged Jess into the boutique. Jess had never felt less like examining lingerie.

'Look at this amazing bra!' raved Flora, plunging recklessly into the merchandise.

She had a weakness for pretty underwear – something Jess couldn't really share. And right now, all Jess could think of was where Fred had gone. She desperately needed to see him on his own, to end this horrible icy feeling that had developed between them. She hadn't even done anything wrong. OK, so the boys were giving him a rough time, but that wasn't her fault. It was as if he was blaming her for their stupid antics.

'The green or the blue?' asked Flora, holding a slinky vest up against her face.

'The blue,' said Jess automatically. She sighed.

'What's wrong, babe?' asked Flora, but rather irritably, as if there was still something wrong left over from earlier. 'Are you still worrying about Chaos? Just give it a rest for an hour or two.'

'I just wish you could get Jack and George to stop taking the piss,' said Jess. 'Fred's gone really strange and he's treating me like dirt suddenly, for no reason.'

'Oh, he just needs to lighten up!' Flora shook her head as if a fly was buzzing around her face. 'OK, the guys are a bit naughty, but they don't mean anything by it. In fact, George told me he thinks Fred is a legend.'

'Well, I don't think Fred realises that,' said Jess doubtfully. 'I think he thinks they think he's a prat.'

'I think that you think that they think that he thinks that . . . whoops! No, I've lost it. Hey! Think about something else for a while. Try this on – it'd look great on you.' Flora gathered up her energy and seemed determined to see the funny side of things and at all costs move on to another subject of conversation.

'No thanks.' Jess wasn't in the mood for shopping. She just lounged around while Flora tried on fifteen different bras and ended up not buying any of them.

The boutique owner looked rather grumpy when they went out without spending any money. Jess knew how she felt – Phil, Dad's ex-partner who'd owned the boutique in St Ives, had often grumbled if he'd had a couple of time-wasters in, trying on loads of stuff and then not buying anything. Jess wondered fleetingly how Dad was and whether he was looking for somewhere to live. If he'd only move out and let Mum get on with her life! It would be really odd, but nice, if he found somewhere to live nearby.

Knowing that Fred was at the internet cafe made Jess restless. She could feel the invisible tug of her tall gawky boy with the mysterious grey eyes.

'Let's go to the internet cafe,' she said as they strolled down the street. 'I need to check my emails. And my cousin said she was going to Facebook me.'

'Fine!' smiled Flora.

As they headed towards the cafe, Jess's mind raced through a number of hopeful scenarios. She was sure they'd find Fred there, and maybe he'd smile at her, properly this time, with a real smile, not that horrible faux grin he'd been using since they arrived, and maybe he'd crack a few jokes and put his arm round her. Maybe he'd have bonded with the other guys and they would have realised how funny he was.

They arrived at the internet cafe, and they found George and Jack there, seated at adjoining PCs. But no Fred.

'Oh, Jess.' George looked up and caught her eye. 'Fredianus said he had to go. He got a text message about a possible band for the dinner dance or some-thing – that event you're organising – and he needed to go back home. He said he'd call you.'

Jess's heart leapt. A possible band! Maybe the tide had turned and things were going to go right for them at last. Of course it was a shock that Fred had gone home, just like that, but if it meant that they'd got a really good band lined up for Chaos it would be worth it.

She felt her phone vibrate in her pocket. Her heart gave a leap. This must be from Fred, to explain the details of the situation. But no! It was from Mum.

WEATHER FORECAST SAYS IT'S GOING TO SNOW. MAKE SURE YOU KEEP WARM AND DON'T GO OFF ON ANY FOOLISH HEROIC EXPEDITIONS. LOVE, MUM X

'So,' said George tauntingly, 'what's he got to say for himself? Is he telling you to watch your step while he's gone? Because, you know, Humph has got the hots for you, big-time!'

Jack, Flora and George all cracked up, as if it was the most ridiculous idea in the world that Humph should get the hots for anybody, let alone Jess. Jess had an uneasy feeling that now Fred had jumped ship, the butt of all their jokes would be her.

Chapter 26

'Oh, it's not Fred,' Jess said with a light, dismissive laugh. 'Only my mum fussing!' She pulled a disgusted face.

'God, I'm starving!' said George, logging off and getting up. 'What say we find the nearest cafe and binge on burger and chips till we explode?'

'Don't forget Tom's a vegetarian, though,' Jack reminded him. 'He'll want to load up with goddam chickpeas and beans and whatever.'

'Hey!' George's eyes lit up. 'Let's all eat some really heavy-duty gas-producing stuff for lunch! Then we can go down to the beach tonight and set fire to our farts! The sky will be lit up! Weymouth will think it's a firework display!'

'Lentil soup!' suggested Jack. 'Baked beans! Where's the nearest vegetarian cafe?'

'Stop it, guys!' giggled Flora helplessly. 'You're totally gross!' She didn't look as if she minded much, though.

Swiftly, Jess checked her emails. Although she knew Fred must be at Weymouth station or even on a train by now, she had a stupid idea that, by magic, he would have managed to send her an email already – via his bionic finger. Failing that, there would be another episode of *Lord of the Wrongs*.

But there was nothing from Dad. In fact, there was nothing much at all. Her cousin Kim in Australia had Facebooked her about some photos of a barbecue they'd had. Everyone was standing around in shorts – amazing to think it was summer there. Australia – the other side of the earth.

Jess had a brief hallucination about the world, this beautiful blue and white planet rolling through space, covered with forests and mountains and beaches and thronged with lovely animals and fishes and birds. She thought the human race should be crazy with joy to have such a sublime place to live, but instead it spent all its time bickering over totally insignificant things.

'Come on, Jess.' Flora tapped her on the shoulder. 'We're going to find a veggie cafe so the guys can stock up with ammunition.'

'OK,' said Jess, 'I've only got two minutes left anyway.' Briefly she checked her mail one last time. There were no new messages. She was really irritated to find that she was still hoping for a message from Fred – that was so pathetic, like believing in fairies.

As George drove them home after a lunch of vegetable curry, stuffed peppers, butter-bean bake and lentil soup (and that was just George's portion), Jess realised that, in fact, Fred could have sent her an email perfectly easily – after all, he'd been at the internet cafe, too, apparently. He could have sent her something – just a line before he left – to explain what was going on and to apologise about having to leave so suddenly. But there was nothing.

She'd sent him a text message during lunch: HEY, WHAT'S ALL THIS ABT A BAND? IS OUR LUCK CHANGING AT LAST? DETAILS ASAP! WISH YOU WERE HERE X

It was now two hours since she'd sent that message, and there still hadn't been any reply. She checked her phone again, for the seventeenth time, even though she hadn't felt it vibrate and knew there wouldn't be anything. Then somehow her mood changed and she felt really fed up with herself for being so clingy. She was going to enjoy the rest of the weekend, Fred or no Fred. And knowing he'd gone off to fix things, like Superman, meant she could relax a bit more. In theory. And she wasn't going to check her phone again until bedtime.

By ten o'clock that evening, she had checked her phone approximately seven hundred times, and there still wasn't a message from Fred. What on earth was going on? Why couldn't he just send the briefest message, to reassure her? To hell with him! Now she *really* wasn't going to check her phone again, or even think about him any more. Despite her decision to forget Fred and just enjoy herself, she had wasted the whole afternoon wondering where he was, why he'd gone and what was happening.

They'd spent the evening playing charades round the fire, and Jess couldn't help thinking how much Fred would have enjoyed that, and been good at it – much better than George and Co. Then, to round off the evening, they'd gone down to the beach and the guys had set fire to their farts. Gross and base though this was, Jess had managed to laugh a few times, because it was quite funny in a revolting way.

'Have you still not heard from Fred?' asked Flora, folding up her sweater. She always folded her clothes and put them away tidily at night – Jess just chucked hers on the floor. Jess was already in her bed, staring at the ceiling. There was a zigzag crack in the paint, shaped like a bolt of lightning.

'No,' Jess sighed.

'I expect he's just out of credit or something,' said Flora, sitting on her bed and looking concerned. She was wearing a Donald Duck nightie, which was working against a serious heart-to-heart somehow. Jess didn't have the heart for a heart-to-heart anyway.

'Yeah, he's so disorganised,' Jess admitted. 'Like me.' As she said it she realised, with a faint sickening twinge, how stupid it had been for two such disorganised people to decide to organise a dinner dance – they'd been carried away on a wave of sympathy for the starving African children.

'I hope the guys didn't get on Fred's nerves too much,' said Flora tentatively. 'Jack's OK really, he'd never mean any harm . . . but George never stops taking the piss.'

'Oh no, I'm sure Fred was fine about that,' Jess hastily reassured her – even though, in the pit of her stomach, there was still a horrid little twinge. She recognised what Flora was saying – indeed the same thought had occurred to her, though she had tried

217

instantly to banish the possibility from her mind. 'He probably got a message from Mackenzie about some band he'd managed to find, and Fred thought he ought to go back right away and meet them and hear them play or whatever.'

'I felt a bit awkward about Fred going off like that,' murmured Flora as she got into bed. 'Because of Mrs Stevens, you know – this weekend is a big deal for them, because of their anniversary.'

'Oh God!' gasped Jess. 'I hadn't thought of that! Is she annoyed about it?'

'She seemed completely nice and understanding,' said Flora. 'But somehow that made it worse.' She snuggled down in her bed and gave Jess a rather accusing glance. Jess could see how Fred's sudden disappearance had put Flora in an awkward position, and she hadn't realised, till now, how it affected anyone apart from herself.

'Oh God, Fred!' she sighed. 'I'll apologise to Mrs Stevens tomorrow and I'll help with the lunch and everything. And if he doesn't send me a text message soon, telling me what's happening, I'll tear him to pieces when we get home.'

'You could start by ripping his pyjamas into tiny shreds,' suggested Flora with a giggle. 'Apparently he left them up in the dorm – and his sponge bag and his books.'

'Typical!' said Jess in exasperation. 'I suppose I'll have to cart all that back home for him. Three Stephen Kings, wasn't it? They must weigh about a ton.'

Fred leaving his stuff behind made Jess feel kind of ashamed. Until now she had nearly always been proud of Fred – of his jokes, his wit, his intelligence. Now she realised his behaviour didn't look good – not just to her and Flora, but to his hosts. If only he would ring! This was turning out to be an uncomfortable weekend. When she finally, finally managed to drift off to sleep, she dreamed of landslides and houses collapsing.

'Hey, Jess – it's snowing!'

Flora's excited cry woke Jess up. There was an unearthly light in the room. Jess stared blearily at the window; she saw a white whirl of falling flakes.

'It's amazing!' cried Flora. 'Quick! Let's get dressed!'

Jess scrambled out of bed and dived into her clothes – all of them, layer after layer. This was going to be a Scott of the Antarctic experience. With a heroic effort, Jess left her phone on the bedside table without even looking at it. It was turned off and so was she.

The snow was brilliant, though. Out on the veranda they found George, wrapped in his dressing gown with a college scarf round his neck. He seemed quieter than usual. They surveyed the amazing sight of millions and millions of snowflakes falling on the sea. They obliterated everything; there was no distant curve of coastline, no Weymouth, no horizon, just a mass of blue and white.

'Every snowflake is unique,' said George thoughtfully. Jess remembered that he was studying some kind of science at uni – Mrs Stevens had been rabbiting on about it. This was the first time he had said something serious. 'You know, its structure.'

'Crystals!' said Flora, catching one on her finger and staring at it in fascination. Jess stuck out her tongue and several snowflakes entered her mouth. It was like eating fairies – although not so cruel, obviously.

'Is that what you're into, George?' Jess asked.

'Environmental geology,' said George. 'Yeah, rocks and fossils and stuff.' Suddenly Jess realised George wasn't just a joker.

'What kind of job will you have, then?' asked Flora.

'Oh, doing boring things,' said George, yawning and stretching. 'You know, uh . . . maybe working out how to deal with flooding or erosion. Or how to manage pollution. It's kind of . . . the interaction between the geosphere – well, the world, really – and human stuff.'

'Cool!' said Flora. But George evidently didn't feel like talking about it any more. He turned to go in, but paused briefly and looked at Jess.

'Jess,' he said, 'I'm sorry if we got on Fred's tits a bit too much, you know. We're just incredibly childish at times, I'm afraid.'

'No, no,' said Jess hastily, 'it was fine. Everything was fine. Fred's just gone to sort some music out for our dinner dance. Don't worry. We were having a bit of a crisis about it – that's why he had to leave so suddenly.'

'OK, well . . . uh, good.' George paused a second longer, sniffed and then went back indoors.

After a humongous fry-up of bacon, eggs, tomatoes, mushrooms and potatoes, and a very thorough washing-up session to placate Mrs Stevens, they all raced down to the beach. Gubbins trotted beside

221

them. He'd never seen the snow before, and kept jumping up and attacking it. There was a snowball fight with the waves crashing in the background; George threw snowballs at Gubbins, then he threw Gubbins around, then he threw sticks at him.

Jess watched, thinking, *He's not just a jerk, he's an environmental geologist.* If he was going to spend his life working on those really mega issues – helping to save the planet, literally – surely he was entitled to a few little practical jokes in his free time? Though she didn't really go for his brand of humour, it wasn't actually evil or anything.

Jess took loads of photos with her phone – which, incidentally, hadn't received any more texts except one from Mum which simply said: **MARTIN AND I ARE AT THE ARBORETUM!** It seemed Mum had struck lucky at last with the half-gorgeous Martin, just at the very moment when Jess's love life had shrivelled away into nothing. Jess wasn't sure whether she was longing to get home again, or dreading it.

Chapter 27

Jess got back home on Sunday evening. There had been room for her in the Stevenses' people carrier because Humph had gone off, hitching, to see his uncle in Bristol, or something. There had been absolutely no message from Fred at all, just a howling silence. The only way to sort this out was to go round to Fred's and grab him. Anyway, she had to return his bag with his pyjamas, sponge bag and books.

He was the great escaper – phone on voicemail, emails ignored, texts unanswered. Jess was raging. If he had indeed managed to fix up a band – for, oh God, next Saturday! – she would forgive him. But she couldn't leave it till tomorrow at school: it had to be now, Sunday night, even though it was quite late and the darkness made it seem even later. She put her trainers on and sped through the night – in a knock-kneed, porky kind of way, admittedly.

It was nine thirty when she reached the Parsonses' house. Fred's family usually stayed up late; his dad was often glued to his beloved football till midnight. Jess rang the doorbell and prepared a polite, business-like smile, because she knew Fred would not be the one to answer the door. As expected, it was Mrs Parsons who did the honours.

'Oh, hi, Jess! Come in! Isn't it cold? How are you? How's your mum?'

Fred's mum couldn't have been nicer. She was always so motherly towards Jess, and seemed to think that she was a good influence on Fred. Ha! Little did she know that Jess's influence on Fred had shrunk to absolute zero. Jess stepped inside. The familiar sound of football drifted out of the sitting room.

'Let me take your coat,' said Fred's mum, her fluffy hair shining in the hall light, her friendly blue eyes twinkling. 'Did you have a lovely time in Dorset? Fred said it was brilliant.' Jess was surprised. Fred had said it was brilliant? What a liar! 'He said you were partying all last night,' said Mrs Parsons with a merry laugh. 'No wonder he looked so shattered when he got back. He was asleep on the sofa for a couple of hours this afternoon.' Partying all night?

If Fred had been partying all night, it certainly hadn't been in Dorset. Jess gritted her teeth and tried to carry on smiling.

'When did he get back?' asked Jess lightly. 'I came back a bit later with the Stevenses.'

'Oh?' Mrs Parsons looked confused. 'Fred turned up about lunchtime today. He's upstairs trying to finish off his homework. Fred! Fre-e-e-ed!' she called up the stairs.

Lunchtime today! Jess's brain reeled. Where had Fred been for those twenty-four hours? More than twenty-four, actually. Had he been sorting out stuff for Chaos? If so, she could forgive him. Just.

'I need to have a word with him about the dinner dance,' said Jess.

'Fine!' beamed Fred's mum. There was a muffled thump from upstairs, the sound of a bedroom door opening and Fred appeared at the top of the stairs, looking pale and shocked. 'Jess has come to see you,' his mum informed him. 'Is your room fit to entertain a lady?'

'What lady?' Fred raised his eyebrows in what was supposed to be a comic pose, but it had no conviction.

'Oh, take no notice, Jess!' laughed Mrs P, who hadn't noticed the undertone of awkwardness. 'Go on up! If you want a hot choc or something, tell Fred to come down and make you one. I'm trying to encourage hospitable behaviour!'

Jess stared up at Fred. He looked about as hospitable as a deer who has spotted a tiger on the horizon. As Jess climbed up towards him, he sort of flinched and stood aside.

'Do you want a hot chocolate?' he asked, catching her eye for a horrible moment – horrible, because there was nothing in his expression but terror and confusion.

'No,' said Jess softly. 'This won't take a minute. I just want a quick word.'

She went through into Fred's bedroom. He followed and shut the door. Usually this manoeuvre was followed by some light-hearted amorous stuff, but today Fred stood back, and the empty air between them made the whole bedroom seem cold and threatening.

'So,' said Jess, turning and facing him. 'What happened? Why didn't you answer my texts? Did you fix up a band? And where were you last night while I was allegedly "partying all night"?'

'I stayed at Mackenzie's,' muttered Fred, looking sheepish and kicking an imaginary sock about. 'On his floor – no mattress, on just the bare boards. He hasn't got a carpet because of his dust allergy. It was like sleeping on concrete. I got, like, five minutes' sleep.'

'Why didn't you come home?' asked Jess, though she suspected she knew the answer.

'I've got no guts at all.' Suddenly Fred looked right into her eyes, and shrugged. 'No need for the parents to know their son is a coward and will be shot for desertion.'

'You're not necessarily going to be shot for desertion,' said Jess carefully. 'Not if you and Mackenzie really did crack the music problem. Presumably you spent all night researching bands?'

'No,' admitted Fred, putting his hands in his pockets and kicking the imaginary sock again. 'We did try for a while, but it was hopeless. So we had to cheer ourselves up by playing computer games.'

'Computer games?' hissed Jess, exploding with anger. 'Fred! You told George you were coming home early to sort out the band!'

'Well, I had to say something.' Fred looked shiftily at the floor. 'I could hardly tell him I'd got sick of their stupid macho messing about and that, yes, I was the spineless nerd they had suspected.' Jess's heart gave another huge dismayed lurch. So Fred hadn't come back to fix the music up at all! He'd left because he just couldn't hack it!

'Fred! They liked you, you idiot! They didn't think you were a spineless nerd! They thought you were really funny! And George said he was sorry if their messing about had got up your nose!'

'Big of him,' said Fred sourly.

'But, anyway, that's not the important thing!' Jess raced on. 'In six days' time a huge crowd of people is going to turn up at St Mark's Church Hall, ready for a good time, and because we've taken their money, we've got to lay it on for them! So what are we going to do about the music? You promised to sort it, remember?'

Fred shrugged. 'Goldilocks have dumped on me again,' he murmured. 'How about Poisonous Trash?'

'No way!' yelled Jess. 'You know Poisonous Trash are rubbish!'

'Ironical, huh?' Fred performed a little ghost of a joke. 'Great name!'

'Fred, this is serious! Parents and uncles and things can't dance to Poisonous Trash! Nobody could dance to them! Nobody could bear to listen to them for a split second! Flora has refused to get up on a stage and sing with them ever again!'

'Well, that's good news, of a sort,' quipped Fred.

'Oh stop it, Fred!' snapped Jess. 'Just be serious for once! We need a band and you said you'd find one.'

Suddenly Fred sat down on his bed. It was as if his long spindly legs had just buckled under him. He leaned back and stared grimly into space.

'I've failed,' he said emptily. 'I did try – slightly. I did ring some bands, really. But they already had gigs . . . I've let you down. You're right. I'm useless. I resign.'

'What do you mean, you resign?' Jess was furious, but had to keep her voice down. She didn't want to upset lovely Mrs Parsons by horrid yelling on a Sunday night.

'I resign from the Chaos committee,' said Fred.

'Committee? What committee? You and me, you mean? So you're just leaving it all to me, then?'

Fred shrugged again. God, he was like a clockwork shrugging machine! Those shoulders were up and down so often they could have generated electricity.

'I still think we should cancel,' he repeated dolefully. 'It's the only sensible thing to do.'

'Fred, we can't just do that!'

'Why not? We could give people their money back. We could say it had to be cancelled due to

229

unforeseen circumstances, like I said before.'

'Yes,' seethed Jess. 'The mysterious absence of a backbone.'

'Quite true.' Fred almost smiled, maddeningly, as if he didn't really care what she thought any more. 'Cancelled due to illness, if you like – absence of a pulse. You decide.'

'Oh yes, convenient, isn't it – letting me decide all the time!'

'Well, it was your idea originally,' said Fred, sidling away from any responsibility even for the concept. 'I just went along with it.'

'God! I don't believe this! How can you be so totally useless?' cried Jess. 'You can resign from organising it if you like, but I'm going to go ahead. We owe it to Oxfam. I'm not going to have starving kids on my conscience. I'll organise the goddam music, the food, the lot! And it's going to be such a mega success, you'll be ashamed you bailed out on it. It'll make you wish you'd never been born.'

'I already wish I'd never been born,' said Fred gloomily.

'Oh, spare me your self-pity!' snapped Jess. She headed for the door.

'Wait!' said Fred, lurching up off the bed. 'I'll see

230

you at school tomorrow anyway, right?'

'My eyes may in some vague way register your presence,' sneered Jess, 'but I shall be far too busy trying to sort out this mess to spend any time with invertebrates.'

Softly, she slammed his door; gently, she stomped down the stairs and grabbed her coat; discreetly and with velvety care, she closed the front door behind her; cautiously, she stepped out on to the icy, iron pavement. And then she burst into tears.

Chapter 28

Home now – and as fast as possible. Thank goodness it was dark so nobody could see her crying. After about five minutes, though, Jess seemed to get through her pain and arrive at an angry place in her head, which felt much better. Instead of being devastated that Fred had let her down so badly and didn't seem to care, she started to plan the best possible revenge.

She would rustle up the most fantastic hosting routine ever seen. Fred had shown himself to be completely spineless, so she'd do the whole thing entirely on her own. The hosting routine would be brilliant, pure comedy gold. But she didn't have much time, because, of course, she also had to organise every other aspect of the goddam dinner dance, at lightning speed and single-handedly. Jess was determined, and in a peculiar way it was almost a relief to know that it was entirely up to her now that Fred was out of the frame.

When she arrived home, the grown-ups were all sitting around the kitchen table: Mum, Dad, Martin and Granny. Mum looked relaxed, thank God, and even Granny seemed to radiate benevolence – maybe she had given up on the hopeless task of trying to organise a reconciliation between Mum and Dad.

'No,' Dad was insisting, 'it must have been 1992, because that was the year I strained my shoulder looking at the moon.'

Mum was laughing, and Martin was refilling her wine glass in an attentive kind of way. Mum locked eyes with Jess, and suddenly looked concerned.

'What's the matter, love?' she cried. Oh God! Jess's mascara must have run, making her look like a panda.

'Nothing,' said Jess, heading out right away. She didn't want Martin to see her looking like this.

'Wait!' Mum jumped up. 'What is it? What's happened?'

'Fred,' Jess blurted out. Then a huge wave of despair hit her, almost like a wave of the sea buckling her knees, and she dropped into the nearest chair and gave a huge, shuddering sigh. 'He's basically just copped out of the dinner dance thing and left me to deal with the whole mess.'

'Why is it a mess?' asked Mum alertly. Jess sighed again.

'I feel so stupid . . . We haven't organised it properly. We didn't get things done in time. Basically we haven't got any catering sorted yet or any bands lined up. Fred said he'd got a band, then he admitted he hadn't, then he – oh, anyway, because it's Valentine's they're all booked already.'

'But this is next Saturday, Jess!' gasped Mum, clutching her face in a semi-hysterical way.

'Yes,' said Jess. An enormous fatigue seemed to creep over her. 'Fred said we ought to cancel it.'

Mum looked thoughtful. 'That's an option, I suppose,' she pondered. 'But, Jess, why on earth didn't you tell me?'

'I didn't want you to know what an idiot I am. I wanted to do it on my own and make you proud of me. I didn't want to come running back to you for support, like some needy little kid. This is the worst evening of my life!' Jess sank down into her sweater, pulling the chunky collar up around her face.

'Uh, Jess,' said Martin, his head cocked on one

side and his eyebrows raised, 'did you say you hadn't got any music?'

'Well, we've got a DJ, but he's not brilliant, and we really wanted to have a proper band so the DJ could just take over in their breaks. I mean, you've got to have a band at a dinner dance, right? And it's not just music for teenagers – it's a family event. Fred said he'd organise a band and he hasn't. I don't even know what he did, or which bands he asked, and he's just completely given up and left everything to me.'

'Well . . . it's probably not your sort of thing, but I play in a band,' Martin confessed shyly, rubbing his head and looking embarrassed. 'It's probably too old fogeyish for what you have in mind, but we play jazz . . . and other things, too.'

'Really?' Jess's heart gave a feeble little skip of hope. 'Jazz! That's what we wanted! Could you . . . would you . . . are you free on the fourteenth?'

'Yes, we are, as a matter of fact,' said Martin. 'We didn't fix up any gigs on Valentine's this year because our singer's daughter is getting married, so the singer wouldn't be available. But we could probably do enough instrumental numbers to get you through the evening – slow smoochy ones and some uptempo stuff – we're quite versatile really. But I'd have to call the other guys and see if they're available.'

'Use the landline!' cried Mum in rapture, gazing adoringly at Martin – he was clearly the nearest thing to Superman available locally. 'In fact, why don't you go upstairs and use my study!' Eagerly she ushered him out of the kitchen.

Granny came up to Jess and placed a gentle hand on her shoulder. 'Cake?' she enquired softly.

'Thanks, Granny, but this is too big a crisis to be solved by cake,' sighed Jess. 'No, I've changed my mind – gimme a massive slice the size of a sofa!'

Speedily Granny did the honours and placed a huge slice of lemon drizzle cake in front of Jess.

'It's one of Deborah's signature cakes,' said Granny proudly.

Jess opened her jaws. Intense, magical, sensational lemonyness exploded in her mouth.

'Oh my God!' raved Jess, spraying cake crumbs everywhere. 'Never mind the dinner dance! I'm going to elope with this cake! Where did Deborah learn to bake like this?'

'Oh, she was a pâtissière, dear,' said Granny. 'She was what they call a station chef at the Queen's Hotel for years. She still turns out for them if there's a crisis.'

'What about our crisis?' asked Dad. 'Could

Deborah save Jess's bacon? What's the catering situation, Jess?'

'Desperate,' admitted Jess. 'I thought I might have to just get a lorryload of ready meals from the supermarket.'

'Hmm,' said Dad, frowning doubtfully. 'Doesn't quite sound good enough for a dinner dance, does it? Do you think Deborah could organise something, Granny?'

'I don't know whether she could take on anything so big,' frowned Granny, shaking her head doubtfully. 'How many people are coming, Jess?'

'Ninety-two, at the last count,' said Jess, pulling an anguished face.

'Hmmm,' Granny mused, 'that sounds like an awful lot to me. Deb's only a pâtissière – she specialises in baked goods and pastries and so on.'

'So let's have pastry wall-to-wall!' yelled Jess. 'Please, please, at least ask her, Granny.'

'Not now,' said Granny firmly. 'It's past Deb's bedtime. But I will call her first thing in the morning.'

'Excellent!' cried Jess, crossing her fingers. 'And if she needs help I'm sure I can find people to give her a hand.'

'Now, sweetheart.' Dad rubbed his face in a thoughtful way. 'Have you fixed up the lighting?'

'Lighting?' Jess's heart missed a beat. 'What lighting? Do I need lighting? I mean, uhh, there's lighting in the hall, surely, isn't there?'

Dad smiled indulgently. 'What, a few light bulbs in the ceiling?' he asked satirically. 'Do you want your dinner dance to have all the atmosphere of a groove down the morgue? You want lasers; you want gobos, strobes, mirror balls; you want fibre optics, dance-floor lighting . . .' Jess was stunned, and could only gawp at her aged parent's unexpected mastery of an art she had so far completely overlooked.

'Tim, Tim!' Granny laughed. 'Don't get carried away! What's your budget for lighting, Jess?'

'Er, pass,' said Jess, cringing at the familiar revelation that her brilliant organisational skills had not included the novel concept of budgeting.

'Don't worry about it!' cried Dad cheerfully. 'This is on me! I've got a friend who runs an events lighting business, and he owes me a favour. As soon as Martin's off the phone I'll give Jim a call. And don't forget I was a lighting designer for dozens of shows when I was at uni.'

'That's news to me, Dad!' said Jess teasingly. 'I

thought you just spent your time getting wasted and looking at the stars!'

At this moment Martin came back into the kitchen from phoning his band members. 'What do you want – the good news or the bad news?' he asked, looking mischievous. Jess reckoned that if the bad news was really bad, he wouldn't have been so perky.

'The bad news first, to get it out of the way,' she said, folding her hands feverishly in prayer.

'Don can't make it – he's the trumpeter. And Ian's busy, too – he's the trombonist. But we'll still have piano, drums, bass and sax. We're normally called The Martin Davies Sextet because there are six of us, so because we'll only be four maybe we could call ourselves The Martin Davies Undersextet.'

'Brilliant!' cried Jess, jumping up and down and pumping the air as if she had won Wimbledon. 'Re-sult!'

It really did feel like a triumph, even if it was the parents who had ridden to the rescue like the US Cavalry in cowboy films. The terrible icy dread which had been rising, like dangerous floodwaters threatening to drown her, had receded. The music was sorted, the lighting was sorted, and though the food was still not organised, perhaps it was the one aspect of the evening which could be improvised by amateurs. She wanted to hug everybody in a huge frenzy of relief and thanks.

But though her terrible icy dread was gone, Jess had another, different bad feeling buried beneath all her relief, and once she went up to bed this other black, gloomy sensation spread through her veins. Fred had let her down so badly, it was as if he really didn't care for her. OK, they'd had rows in the past, but she'd never really doubted that he cared. This time she felt he'd abandoned her to the wolves, and run like hell to save his own skin. Thank God they'd never gone on safari together. Fred was always joking, in a self-deprecating way, that he hadn't got a backbone. But somehow he'd always made up for it and convinced her that he was, though maddening, kind of irresistible.

This time she had an awful sickening sense that the way he'd let her down, first in Dorset, and more significantly over the dinner dance organisation, showed a real, horrible flaw in his character. She couldn't depend on him, and that made her feel that perhaps he wasn't so very irresistible after all. He wasn't just letting her down – he was letting himself down. Fred should have been better than this.

What was he feeling now? Her finger itched to send him a triumphant text telling him that she'd sorted it. But as Fred might be suffering a certain amount of agony – at least, she hoped so – it seemed only right to allow him to go on suffering it for a little while longer. Besides, he'd 'resigned', so really it was none of his business any more. Jess was beginning to enjoy the feeling of independence and progress. She'd show him! As she drifted off to sleep, she began to develop some ideas about how to host Chaos, maybe as a postmodern Cinderella . . .

Chapter 29

School was going to be difficult. Jess hadn't slept well and got up early to disguise the bags under her eyes and re-pluck her eyebrows. She wasn't going to speak to Fred, obviously; in fact, she wouldn't even look vaguely in his direction if she could help it. But if he looked at her, she wanted him to be stunned by her magnificent, cruel beauty. As a cosmetics project it was a huge challenge, since currently she looked like a hamster who has gone ten rounds with a Jack Russell terrier.

Jess had been dreading seeing Fred, but at least she had sorted most of Chaos so she felt she could face all her friends who had bought tickets – before, she'd been feeling so guilty, it was as if she'd secretly murdered somebody they loved and hidden the body under her patio. However, as she approached the school gates, looking as magnificent and cruel as possible, Gemma Fawcett ran up. She was a small girl with a straight black shiny bob which Jess had always admired. If only her own hair would agree to hang quietly in one direction, instead of sticking up here and there randomly all over her head like a neglected vegetable plot in winter.

'Jess!' cried Gemma. 'We can't come to Chaos after all! My dad broke his ankle! Can we have our money back?'

Jess hadn't anticipated this kind of thing. She forgot, for a moment, to look magnificent and cruel and instead became a limp, gibbering puppet on invisible tangled strings. 'Er, I'm not sure . . . uh, I suppose so . . . um, urgh . . .'

Gemma thrust four tickets into Jess's shaking hand. 'Can you let me have a full refund today?' she demanded, her perfect black bob gleaming glossily in the morning light. Jess was beginning to hate Gemma's hair. She was making plans to smuggle a ball of recently chewed gum into it at the earliest opportunity.

'Well . . . you see, the money's in the bank and I haven't got the chequebook with me.' Jess hesitated. Gemma looked cross and surprised.

'My mum said, like, you'd have to give us a full refund because it's not for another five days and you'll be able to sell the tickets to somebody else, right?'

'Yes, of course!' Jess nodded emphatically, as if this was something she dealt with every hour, even though the idea of reselling the tickets to somebody else hadn't even occurred to her. 'I could probably bring a cheque round tonight,' she suggested feebly. 'Where do you live?'

'Little Granscombe,' said Gemma. 'It's way out in the country past the mall.'

'Oh, er . . .' Jess was still struggling to stay polite. 'How about if I bring the cheque to school tomorrow?'

'Hmmm.' Gemma sounded doubtful. She pursed her lips – suddenly Jess realised that Gemma's lips were rather horrid and pouty. She was going to pout big-time when she discovered that ball of chewing gum in her hair. 'I'll call my mum at lunchtime and ask. Maybe you should give us an IOU.'

Jess's temper almost snapped, but she knew it was important to keep customers happy. As she ripped open her school bag to find a scrap of paper, she vowed she would never again in her entire life

244

organise anything or sell anything. A majorly terrifying thought hit her: what if Martin's band was crap and Dad's lighting blew a fuse and the buffet – wherever that was going to come from – gave everybody food poisoning? Would they all ask for their money back?

Jess tore a page out of her rough book, scribbled *I owe Gemma Fawcett £150, Jess Jordan*, then handed it over. Gemma looked at it suspiciously.

'It looks a bit scrappy,' she commented disdainfully.

'Don't worry,' snarled Jess. 'I'll give you another one at lunchtime on gold embossed paper, delivered on a red plush cushion by a freakin' footman in a wig and tights!' Then she stalked off, leaving Gemma open-mouthed. This was the best moment of the day so far.

Jess was late for registration, and entered the classroom looking magnificent and cruel. Flora had bagged the best radiator under a window, so Jess joined her, ignoring everybody else, and sat down cruelly and magnificently. Fred was going to grovel before her grandeur!

While Mr Fothergill droned through a few announcements, Flora leaned in close to Jess's ear and whispered, 'Fred's away. Mackenzie says he's got flu!'

Jess felt a lurch of something: disappointment, concern and then disbelief. Fred wasn't here? Suddenly the room felt a very different place. He had the flu? Oh yeah? Or was he just faking it because he didn't have the nerve to face her? She shot Flora a sceptical eyebrow and sighed deeply. How absolutely typical. Still, at least she didn't have to be magnificent and cruel all the time, thank God. It was hard work.

At break a few people gathered round Jess to hear the latest Chaos details.

'So, what's the name of this band again?' asked Flora, who was deeply relieved that Poisonous Trash was not going to be resurrected.

'It's The Martin Davies Undersextet,' said Jess.

'Are they undersexed?' asked Mackenzie predictably.

'They're all about forty,' said Jess, smiling. 'So I expect they've completely given up on all that.'

'How are you going to manage, now Fred's got the flu?' demanded Jodie melodramatically.

'Oh, no problem!' Jess assured her breezily. 'I was organising the whole thing anyway. Admin isn't Fred's strong point.' She wanted to keep things light and casual. Nobody must know that she and Fred had had that terrible bust-up. Nobody except Flora, that is.

'But what about the hosting?' Jodie persisted. 'Wasn't it going to be a double act? Fred's so hilarious!'

'Well, sorry, but you're just going to have to manage with boring old me!' Jess was trying hard to keep her temper again.

'You're gonna have a lot on your plate,' said Ben Jones quietly. 'Is there anything I could do to help?'

'I thought you'd bought tickets, Ben?' pounced Jodie, who had already spent many hours speculating which lucky girl was going to be escorted to Chaos by the divine Ben.

'Yeah, I've bought tickets and stuff, but I don't mind helping as well,' said Ben casually. 'I could, um, be on the door if you like?' His magical blue eyes washed over Jess like a Caribbean wave. There had always been a little tiny frisson of something or other between them, once she'd got over the huge crush she had had on him a year ago. But she'd never felt like tiptoeing into that territory, even during Fred's worst moments of foolishness. Ben was, in some ultimate way, kind of vulnerable despite his glamour, and she'd always known, since getting together with Fred, that Ben Jones was not for her. Although now it seemed that Fred might not be for her, either.

'On the door?' gasped Jess. Of course! They needed somebody on the door! This was another thing that she hadn't thought about – and nor had Fred, the lazy toad, lying cosily at home on his sofa pretending to be ill while she toiled over a hot Chaos. 'That would be fabulous!' She smiled gratefully. It would give the whole evening a tremendously stylish quality to have somebody as handsome as Ben Jones checking the tickets. 'What I also need,' Jess went on, trying to look relaxed and confident even though she was treading on thin ice, 'is possibly a bit of help with the buffet?'

'I thought you were getting caterers in?' demanded Jodie.

'Oh yes, of course – we are,' lied Jess hastily.

'Who are they?' asked Jodie. Jess couldn't help thinking that Jodie's hair, as well as Gemma's, might benefit from some chewing gum.

'It's a new company,' said Jess, casting around desperately for a name that would suit an exciting young business venture, 'called, uh, The Eating Machine.'

'Horrid name,' said Jodie. 'They should change it.'

Jess made hasty plans to buy several packs of chewing gum.

At lunchtime, Flora had a music lesson so Jess hid away in a quiet corner of the library and worked on her hosting script. So Fred was 'hilarious', was he? She was going to make damn sure she was twice as hilarious as he had ever been! Her mind was racing with indignation, and she scribbled down masses of ideas.

Cinderella was perfect territory. *I'm not supposed to be here*, she wrote. *I wasn't allowed to go to the ball. My fairy godmother turned up and promised me a makeover, but she's so disorganised – she'd forgotten to charge her wand* . . . There were lots of possible jokes about ugly sisters and pumpkins and mice and glass slippers and that needy nerd Buttons, who was always hanging about . . . Jess was having more fun than she'd had in weeks.

Chapter 30

Jess walked home via Flora's house with Flora and Jack. Because Jack was there, she and Flora couldn't embark on really sensitive subjects.

'How's Fred?' asked Jack.

'Oh, fine,' said Jess, gritting her teeth. 'Although he's got the flu, I expect it's the very best sort. How's George?'

'He's good,' said Jack. 'In fact, he said he might like to come to Chaos if you've got four tickets spare?'

'I'm not sure,' muttered Jess, her heart going into overdrive. If George and the guys were there, they might undermine everything with some stupid stunt. She'd enjoyed working on her script so much at lunchtime that she couldn't bear the thought of being upstaged by those idiots. 'I think we're all sold out, I'm sorry.'

'No, you're not!' exclaimed Flora with a puzzled little frown. 'Didn't you have some tickets left anyway? And you told me Gemma Fawcett returned her four today, so that makes how many . . . ?'

'So would there be six spare?' asked Jack. 'George's girlfriend is at St Benedict's, and Tom wants to bring somebody called Rhiannon.'

'And Humph?' said Jess, accepting the inevitable – the Jackass crowd were coming to ruin her event. They would certainly pull some dreadful stunt to hijack the occasion. 'Does Humph have a girlfriend? It's kind of hard to imagine.'

Jack laughed. 'I'm not sure,' he said. 'He's a bit mysterious . . . maybe he'll come with Gubbins.'

'Six tickets, then?' said Flora enthusiastically. Jess wished Flora would keep her nose out. Having George and Co coming to Chaos revived Jess's feelings of terror and nausea.

'Yeah,' said Jack. 'I'll bring the cheque in tomorrow. That's how much exactly?'

'Over to you, brainbox,' Jess said acidly to Flora.

'Two hundred and twenty-five pounds,' said Flora. 'Big bucks! Oxfam will be thrilled!'

'Wow! Big money talks!' said Jack, putting his arm around Flo and turning to Jess with a smile.

'I'm only after her millions, you know.'

'You're heading for a big disappointment, then,' said Flora. 'My dad's really worried about his business – he said he might go bust before the end of the summer.'

'What?' cried Jess in alarm. 'But I thought your dad's business was rock solid. Everybody needs bathrooms!'

'Hmm,' said Flora, looking a bit serious now. 'Apparently nobody's having bathroom makeovers these days. They're making do with their tired old bathrooms from three years ago.'

'The tight-fisted swine!' exclaimed Jess. 'How dare they? We should break into people's houses at night and trash their bathrooms!' Flora smiled, but only faintly.

'When we bought these tickets Dad said that it would be the last family treat for some time,' added Flora edgily.

'Oh God!' Jess was dismayed. But she wasn't just shocked for Flora, because her comfortable lifestyle might soon come to an end (her big house with all mod cons, her silk-clad mum sprawled on a huge cloudy white sofa, beautiful sisters wearing designer jeans and playing the flute, father sucking indigestion pills while booking holidays in Antigua . . .). Jess also had a more personal concern. If Chaos was to be the Barclay family's last treat for a while, and it turned out to be a five-star fiasco, Mr Barclay would be just the kind of guy to demand his money back – loudly, right there and then, in front of everybody. Jess felt horribly uneasy.

She left Flora and Jack at Flo's house, which now looked strangely forlorn despite the big posh front door and the matching bay trees in pots on either side. Flora had invited her in, but Jess had stuff to do – most importantly she had to get home and ask Granny if Deborah was up for organising the buffet. And she couldn't wait to get cracking on her hosting script again. For a split second she wondered if anyone – not Fred, literally anyone – had sent her a text, so she checked her phone. Nothing.

'Hi, Jess!' She looked up and was startled to see Polly the goth, with her red hair and metal-studded chalky-white face, daughter of Mum's second worst date, Ed the Homophobic Builder. 'Sorry I haven't been in touch,' said Polly. Jess remembered that they had exchanged contact details.

'Oh, sorry I haven't,' said Jess hastily. It was so odd with goths, Jess thought, they look like the scariest monsters from hell, but they're usually incredibly polite and gentle.

'How's your mum?' asked Polly. 'I thought she was really, really nice – much too good for Dad.'

'Oh, I don't know about that,' said Jess with a wry smile. 'I thought your dad was awesome – much too good for Mum!'

'Oh, no, no.' Polly shook her head vigorously, causing a tinkling sound. 'Your mum was really, really interesting, and my dad's stuck with these really Stone Age attitudes, like, you know what he said after our evening?'

'What?' enquired Jess fearfully. She hoped Ed the Builder hadn't said anything insulting about Mum – that was Jess's job.

'He said he thought your mum was really nice,' said Polly, 'but he never felt comfortable with clever women. He said they made him feel inadequate.'

'Well, that's kind of a compliment for Mum,' said Jess, relieved.

'Yes, but it shows how his mind works! He's going out with a shelf-stacker now,' grumbled Polly.

'There's nothing wrong with shelf-stackers,' suggested Jess thoughtfully. She had a feeling that, if her

254

comedy career didn't take off, she might stack shelves herself one day.

'No, I know, but your mum is so interesting! A librarian! She reads all these amazing books! The shelf-stacker just smokes and drinks and watches those TV shopping channels.' Polly gave a contemptuous snort.

'But your dad must believe in educating women,' Jess pointed out, 'because you're at college, right?'

'That's mainly my mum's influence.' Polly shrugged. 'And he just has to accept it. Plus he thinks it's OK because my course is Hospitality Supervision NVQ Level 3 – what he thinks of as women's work. If I wanted to be an astronomer or a surgeon or something, he'd be sneering and making jokes about it all the time.'

'Dads!' sighed Jess with a smile.

'How's your dad?' asked Polly. 'He sounded really cool.'

'He's fine, thanks,' said Jess. She didn't want to go into all that now. There was a brief silence.

'Well, nice meeting you again,' said Polly. Then she hesitated. 'I don't suppose you'd like to come out on Saturday? See a movie or something?'

Jess was tempted. 'That sounds really nice,' she

mused. 'Aaaagh! No! Wait! What am I thinking of? I'm organising a dinner dance on Saturday night!'

'Really?' Polly's eyes widened. 'Where?'

'At St Mark's Church Hall,' said Jess. 'It's called Chaos.'

'I've seen the posters!' Polly nodded in recognition. 'They were great. Who designed them?'

'I did,' admitted Jess, embarrassed.

'God! Well, you're really talented, Jess!' insisted Polly.

Jess shook her head and felt awkward. 'Well, I must go,' she murmured. 'Got loads to do. Nice seeing you.'

'Keep in touch,' Polly beamed. 'Send me a text sometime when you're free and we can hook up, OK?'

'Yeah, that would be great!' Jess grinned. Polly seemed like a really nice person. Once the hell of Chaos was over, maybe they could get together and do something. Though Jess had never wanted to be a goth herself, she quite liked the idea of walking through town with one.

At last she arrived home. As she opened the front door Granny popped out of her room, looking tense.

'Oh, Jess, love!' she exclaimed. 'I thought you'd

never come home! I've got some bad news for you, I'm afraid!'

Instantly Jess's heart lurched up towards her tonsils. 'What? What?' she gasped. Mum dead? Dad dead? Mum and Dad dead? Or – possibly even worse – reconciled?

'Don't worry, dear, nobody's died,' said Granny, clutching Jess's hand.

'Ill?' gasped Jess. 'Injured? Run over?'

'No, no, Jess, nothing like that. Calm down.'

'Well, tell me what it is, then!' yelled Jess. Granny could be infuriating sometimes.

'It's Deborah – I asked her about the dinner dance buffet, but the most she can do would be the desserts, love. Just a couple of cheesecakes and about four fruit flans, she said. I'm so sorry. You must be disappointed.'

Bad though Jess's arithmetic was, even she could see that a couple of cheesecakes and four fruit flans wouldn't go very far towards feeding a hundred. Unless Jesus himself appeared and rolled up his sleeves, when it came to catering, she was going to be in the very depths of doo-doo.

Chapter 31

'Never mind, Granny,' said Jess. She squeezed Granny's arm. 'I'll think of something. Get back to Miss Marple!' She could hear the unmistakable sound of the sleuth's sig tune wafting out from Granny's den. Jess slouched through to the kitchen, her heart heavy as lead.

There was a note on the table in Dad's handwriting: *Jess, lighting sorted, it's going to be terrific! Jim's had a cancellation so we can have the works: mirror ball, the lot. Gone out to buy ingredients for celebration curry. Back soon. Love, Dad x*

Dear Dad! He'd done his best. Chaos was going to look amazing – unless a fuse blew or something. And Martin's band might be really good, because there was something reassuring about Martin, and guys still playing in a band in their forties have had plenty of time to get it right.

Jess's hosting script was sizzling along nicely. But what on earth were the guests going to eat? A couple of fruit flans weren't going to satisfy people who had paid £75 for a double ticket. Jess slumped down in a chair and cradled her head in her hands. The most delicious curry in the world wasn't going to lift her out of despair – not unless it came in ninety-four portions next Saturday night. For a split second she considered asking Dad to do the catering for Chaos. But he was already doing the lighting. And though multi-talented, he wasn't Superman.

Suddenly her mobile rang. It was a number she didn't recognise.

'Hi, Jess?'

'Hello?' She didn't recognise the voice. Some girl – oh please, God, not Gemma Fawcett pestering for a refund.

'It was really nice to see you today.' Not Gemma, obviously – seeing Gemma had been possibly the most unpleasant moment in a day packed with angst. Who the hell else had she seen today? Jess had had so much on her mind that though she ransacked her memory banks, they could not come up with the ID of a single female person she might have seen in the past week.

'Sorry, who is this?' Jess asked impatiently. She so hated people who didn't identify themselves. It was unbelievably big-headed of them just to assume she would know who they were. She detested this person already.

'Sorry, I'm such an idiot. It's Polly.' For a split second even knowing it was 'Polly' didn't help; her mind was still a fog.

'Oh, hi, Polly. Sorry, I'm a bit distracted at the moment,' said Jess. It was Polly the goth!

'Oh, have I rung at an inconvenient moment?' Polly speeded up. 'So sorry, I'll be quick, then. I only rang to ask if there are any tickets left for Chaos? It sounds really, really cool, and I was telling my friends Simon and Jules and Bart about it and we'd really, really like to come.'

'Uh . . .' Jess hesitated. She liked Polly, but how could she sell more tickets for an event that was still lacking the most essential ingredient – grub? 'Polly, I'm not sure I can actually sell you tickets for Chaos,' she faltered. 'It's just . . . you see, I'm having terrible trouble organising the catering. Stupidly, because I am basically a five-star idiot, I left it too late and by the time I started getting in touch with catering companies they were already fully booked. I've messed up big time and I feel like disappearing off the map and getting a job in South America.' Jess felt a wave of relief at having unburdened herself and confessed all, even if it was to a random semi-stranger.

'But, Jess, you should have told me,' said Polly, not sounding disappointed at all – in fact, sounding bizarrely excited.

'I'm telling you now,' said Jess. 'It's going to be a five-star fiasco. There won't be anything to eat.'

'No, listen, Jess – catering, that's what I'm studying, right?' Jess's heart gave a feeble little skip of hope and surprise. 'I told you I'm doing Hospitality Supervision NVQ Level 3, didn't I?'

'Yes,' said Jess blankly. 'Sounds impressive, but what does it mean?'

'It's all about organising events!' enthused Polly. 'Things like your dinner dance! My mates and I would love to do it! What's your budget per head? Give me a couple of hours and I'll come back to you with some menus!'

'My God, my God, my God!' That was all Jess could say for a split second. 'Can you really do this, Polly? Because if you can, you are literally my guardian angel!'

'Of course we can do it,' Polly assured her cheerily.

'It'll be a piece of cake – not literally, of course, but you may want some gateaux for dessert, even though nowadays people find gateaux a bit old-fashioned.'

Briefly Jess and Polly worked out a basic budget – well, Polly worked it out, really, based on the ticket price, while Jess just gawped and made admiring noises. Then Polly rang off, apparently delighted to have been handed this most awful of responsibilities. Jess could only sit in her chair and marvel at how different people were. The thought of having to organise dinner for a hundred people made Jess feel limp with terror, but Polly grabbed the opportunity like a dog pouncing on a juicy bone.

'Thank you, God,' said Jess fervently to the ceiling. Then she grabbed her phone again – she had to call Flora and give her the good news. But not Fred. He could damn well wait. After a conversation with Flora which consisted mainly of high-pitched whooping noises, and after explaining to Granny (with Miss Marple paused over a corpse in a cupboard) just what the whooping signified, Jess ran upstairs, flung off her clothes and had a long, hot shower, singing wildly all the time. She went right through the greatest hits of Freddy Mercury – her Dad's favourite artist, though he hadn't gone *too* far.

Thank God Dad wasn't a Freddy Mercury tribute lookalike . . .

Hmmm – the hosting routine! Jess finished the shower, her mind racing. Five minutes later, dried and dressed, she was crouched over her laptop, working on her stand-up again. It was going brilliantly. Jokes just seemed to crowd into her head. In fact, Jess began to wonder how she was going to fit them all into three or four relatively short appearances. She didn't need much material: just a welcome, an introduction to the band, and then, presumably about an hour later, an invitation to the buffet and, finally, a long goodnight. But it would have to be slick, smart, funny and well-rehearsed. She began to rewrite the script, feeling excited; there were some great jokes here and she couldn't wait to perform it.

She was deep in her rewrite when her mobile rang. It was Polly again.

'OK, Jess, I've got a sample menu here. This is based on a cost of twelve pounds a head, OK?'

'Uh – yes, fine,' agreed Jess. Her head was reeling already.

'Right,' said Polly, 'here we go. This is a hot fork buffet, OK?'

'Of course,' said Jess, though she had a brief hallucination of a hot fork being used as a weapon in some kind of catering skirmish.

'Right,' said Polly importantly. 'I thought we could have a choice of tuna or chicken main course, with pasta or mushroom stroganoff for the veggies. So that would be Basque chicken (chicken with haricot beans and Spanish spiced sausage in tomato sauce) or chargrilled tuna with tabbouleh –'

'With what?' gasped Jess.

'Tabbouleh.'

'What's tabbouleh?'

'It's basically cracked bulgur wheat.'

'What's bulgur?'

'Well, it's a sort of grain thing, with chopped parsley, mint, tomatoes, spring onions – it's yummy!'

'OK,' said Jess faintly. 'Go on.'

'This would come with Charlotte potatoes, right?' Polly ranted on. Jess had never heard of potatoes called Charlotte, but she found the whole thing immensely glamorous.

'Lovely,' she murmured.

'Plus seasonal vegetables and salads,' Polly added. 'Then pear and ginger tart or passion fruit cheesecake, with tea and coffee. Does that sound OK?'

'It sounds wonderful,' groaned Jess. 'But won't it cost a bomb?'

'Oh no,' trilled Polly. 'Like I said, this is based on a cost of twelve pounds a head, without wine, obviously – we can sell that separately.' Jess felt dizzy at the thought of selling wine separately. 'There will be ten of us working on this,' Polly went on briskly. 'We'll do all the prep at college and then come and set it up at the venue. We'll do it for fifty pounds each. Is that OK?' Jess's heart lurched in terror. What was ten times £50? Was it big bucks? Could they afford it?

'Fine!' she squeaked.

'Excellent, excellent,' gabbled Polly. 'This is so exciting, wonderful! I'll call back later with some more details. Bye!'

She rang off. Jess slumped down at the kitchen table. Could she afford to pay Polly's catering friends? What was tabbouleh? What was bulgur? Hell, what was pear and ginger tart? She sneaked into Granny's room and cuddled up on the sofa with her. Somebody on TV was being lavishly murdered with a golf club. Compared with having to organise a dinner dance, it seemed quite an attractive option.

Chapter 32

Eventually Valentine's arrived. There was no card from Fred, but there probably wouldn't have been under normal circumstances anyway. He'd been away all week with the flu, and Fred was such a grouch when it came to conventional things that he probably wouldn't have sent one even if they hadn't had the big bad bust-up. Jess was cross with herself for even thinking about the possibility of a card from him, especially because she was in such a strop with him that she hadn't even considered sending him one. And even if he had sent one, she would have burnt it. It would take more than a piddling valentine card for Fred to get back into her good books.

Mum, Dad and Granny had sent her a card with fluffy animals on – they hadn't signed it but she recognised Dad's lame attempt at disguised handwriting on the envelope and she could tell from their expressions that they were all in on the joke. Although it was nice of them, it hardly fitted the bill, and Jess didn't have time to fret about her rock-bottom sweetheart status. This evening Chaos would unfold – only in one sense of the word, hopefully.

The problem of what to wear had been solved by her Cinderella role. To dress down she'd made a kind of holey net which slipped on over her black stretchy top and footless tights, and there was a piece of elastic which went round her waist, with ragged bits of random cloth hanging down in ripped shreds. On stage she would be barefoot (she'd take her favourite shoes, of course, even though, as they were killer heels, she'd actually be more comfortable when she kicked them off).

It was kind of liberating to be spending the evening literally in rags. As long as her make-up was brilliant it wouldn't matter. Most of the time she'd be circulating with her mates, and obviously she wanted to appear heartbreakingly ravishing in case Fred was there – if he'd managed to force himself off his sofa to turn up and show support. So she spent her usual three hours on her make-up, designing a pair of Cinderella eyebrows emphasising her innocence and poverty but hinting at her royal destiny (Jess was becoming an eyebrow expert). She sprayed some glitter in her hair and painted her nails black (cinders, right?) and then, basically, she was ready to go.

Mum, who would be assisting Ben Jones front of house, drove her to the venue an hour early. Dad, of course, had been there all day fixing the lights which he'd got from his Oxford chum, and Martin had said his band would be there in the afternoon to have a look at the space and rehearse a number or two. Gordon Smith's disco, which would take over in the band's rest breaks, would also be all set up when Jess arrived.

All the same, her heart was hammering as she entered the hall. There was a big banner hanging over the entrance – this had been cooked up in a hurry by Flora and Jodie. It read *CHAOS* and was decorated with hearts and arrows and snowflakes – the usual stuff. Jess secretly prayed that their choice of name for the dinner dance would not prove to be a spooky premonition.

She entered the lobby to find Ben Jones in a tux, looking like a million dollars.

'Oh, hello, Ben, you look very smart,' said Mum, but then she effortlessly looked away to the table where she was going to sit. How could Mum bear to tear her eyes away from such a dazzling sight? Jess marvelled. It must be a generation thing.

Somebody had put up signs showing where the loos were, and there was a little bolt-hole that had been adapted to a cloakroom. There was a girl inside untangling coat hangers.

'This is my cousin Melissa,' said Ben. Jess beamed at her.

'I hadn't realised we'd need a cloakroom!' gasped Jess. 'Thanks so much!'

'No problem,' said Melissa with a cute grin. 'I just hope there's room for a hundred coats in here!'

Jess wondered if Melissa and Ben were an item as well as being cousins. She hoped not somehow. Although she knew that Ben Jones was Not For Her, she didn't really want him to be for anybody else, either. It's the same way one feels about dishy actors or singers – you like to think of them going home to a lonely monastic bed, not romping with horrid bimbos or even perfectly nice other girls who are simply, tragically, Not You.

Jess entered the main hall, and gasped. Dad was up on a ladder fixing some lights, and the place looked amazing. Polly came bustling up. Though she still had a fair amount of metal in her face, she looked very professional in chef's whites and she seemed to have a team of people milling around some trestle tables at the back of the hall, arranging hotplates, bringing in piles of plates and cutlery and so on.

It was amazing to see all these people busily conjuring up her dinner dance – people she'd never even met, all confidently doing their bit. Suddenly she realised it was going to be OK. The DJ had set up his disco corner with coloured lights sweeping across the stage. Martin was up there talking to a thin guy with a shaved head who was doing something to a drum kit.

'You see,' said Mum in her ear, giving her arm a secret squeeze. 'It's all under control!'

Jess heaved a huge, huge sigh.

'I thought around eight thirty would be the best time to serve the food?' asked Polly.

Jess panicked again. The moment of relief had been short-lived. Evidently she still had to make decisions, not to mention perform the hosting routine. A cold thrill of terror ran through her ribcage.

'That would be kind of not too early but not too late,' Polly went on. 'And before that there'll be some

270

dancing and people can buy drinks at the bar. We've put nibbles on every table.'

Jess noticed how nicely the tables had been dressed, with pink and purple paper cloths, and paper butterflies on long bendy wires stuck into a central cluster of little flowers – the butterflies moved slightly in the currents of air. Each table had dishes of olives and nuts, and tiny sparkly confetti hearts were scattered randomly about. Jess wondered how much it had all cost, but Polly assured her that dressing the tables would be included in their fee, and in fact she had a friend, Kylie, who liked doing nothing better.

'I see they've put the bar in the side room,' Mum pointed out.

Jess's heart gave an anxious little skip. Fred's dad had agreed to run the bar, of course. Halfway down the hall, there was a door leading to an extra room where, presumably, Fred's dad would be installed. Jess hoped that he wasn't missing any important football tonight, as a grumpy barman would be a bit of a downer on Valentine's. She wondered, even more urgently, if she should go in there and ask him how Fred was, or at the very least if he was still alive. (Despite everything, this option was preferable.)

'If you go backstage,' said Mum, 'I expect you'll

find a green room where the performers can chill out. I'll go back to the lobby and make sure everything's OK there – people will be arriving soon.'

Jess postponed the chat with Fred's dad and went backstage, entering the green room. A couple of middle-aged men looked up with cheery smiles.

'We're part of The Martin Davies Undersextet,' said a bearded one. 'And you must be Cinderella! I'm afraid there aren't any Prince Charmings here, love.'

Jess smiled, and at that moment Martin came in and introduced everybody. The bearded guy was Bill the saxophone player, and the other guy, who was thin and smiley, was Roy the bass player. The drummer was apparently called Dave.

'I think there's a little dressing room for you, Jess,' said Martin, pointing to a corner. 'You're the star of the show after all.'

'There's a message for you in there,' said Bill with a wink. 'Somebody delivered a card.'

Jess walked into her tiny dressing room. A card was propped against a bottle of water on the dressing table. Jess grabbed it, wondering if it would be from Fred. But it was in a stranger's handwriting. Jess ripped it open. It was a good luck card with a massive silver horseshoe adorned with pale blue satin bows, and it said: *Here's to a great success – you deserve a triumph! Congrats, Martin and the Undersextet.* Jess felt simultaneously grateful to Martin for being so kind, and annoyed that the card wasn't from Fred. Still, she managed to thank them effusively.

Then she wandered into the hall again. She really ought to find out if Fred was here. In a way she hoped he had turned up, so he could be blown away by the brilliance of her hosting routine. On the other hand, if he wasn't here it would kind of be a relief. But she had to know. So she headed for the bar area and found Mr Parsons polishing glasses with his usual slow dignity.

'These glasses are a disgrace,' he informed her sourly, holding one up to the light. That was typical of Fred's dad – no hellos, none of the usual small talk – he always just plunged straight into the important stuff. 'I've half a mind to ask for a refund.'

'A refund?' asked Jess, all at sea. She still hadn't mastered some of the details of organising a dinner dance.

'We hired the glasses from Frobisher's,' commented Fred's dad. 'A rip-off. Don't worry, I'll let them know what I think of them in no uncertain terms.'

'Oh, er, well, good,' spluttered Jess, supposing that

Frobisher's must be punished for their slackness and Mr Parsons was the man for the job. 'Er, how's Fred?' she asked, trying to sound casual. 'Is he here?'

'He's somewhere around.' Mr Parsons shrugged gloomily.

Jess made her way back to the dressing room. Throngs of people were arriving, but she couldn't see Fred anywhere. However, now she knew he was here. She couldn't wait to perform – it would prove to him how fantastically she could do without him. She knew her stand-up script was a winner and she was really looking forward to doing it. It was a kind of treat for her – a reward for not giving up.

Chapter 33

All the same, she was terrified, of course. Jess lurked in her dressing room, chewing her fingernails.

Occasionally she fired off a text to her mum at front of house. **THEY'RE PILING IN!** Mum reported. **EVERYBODY LOOKS STUNNING! JACK'S BRO AND HIS FRIENDS FROM UNI HAVE COME IN DRAG!**

Oh God! Trust George and Co to turn up and try to turn the whole thing into a goddam charade! On the other hand, maybe it wouldn't matter. Maybe it would add to the hilarity of the whole occasion. Jess was dying to take a peep at them, despite all her misgivings. However, she stayed where she was.

There was a knock on her door. Her heart, already hammering with terror, gave a panicky lurch. But it was only Martin.

'In about two minutes,' he said, looking at his

watch, 'when we've finished this number, Dave will do a drum roll and you should just step into position and do your welcome stuff. Your dad's fixed you up with a spotlight, so don't get dazzled and fall off the stage!'

'You're such a spoilsport, Martin,' quipped Jess. 'How else are we going to get the evening off to a flying start? The band sounds absolutely great, by the way.'

Martin smiled. 'We're not bad for veterans,' he said. 'I must get back onstage – I've got a piano solo coming up.'

He disappeared, and Jess followed, kicking off her shoes and mussing up her hair (result: sparkly hands, but it all seemed to add to the Cinderella look).

She waited in the wings, stage left, her heart hammering even harder. The band's number finished and straight away there was a drum roll. Whole bucketfuls of adrenalin surged up Jess's neck. She stepped forward into a pool of light. Now she could see nothing.

'Please, please!' she said in a plaintive Cinderella voice. 'Ladies and gentlemen, don't tell anybody I'm at the ball! I'm not supposed to be here! My ugly sisters are here somewhere – ah, there they are . . .'

She peered randomly into the blackness. 'Oh no, sorry, madam, the light is so poor in here!' This got a laugh, the first one of the evening – always a relief. The audience seemed to be determined to enjoy themselves, which is good news for a comedian.

'I was supposed to stay at home chopping up rats for the ratatouille,' Jess went on, to more laughter. 'But I couldn't resist creeping in through the back door, because I wanted to catch a glimpse of Prince Charming! Oh, he makes my little heart go pit-a-pat!' Jess took up a fragile doting pose, hands clasped in adoration at the very thought of royalty. 'Has anyone seen him yet?'

'He's at Boujis!' shouted a voice from the back of the room. Boujis is, of course, the fave nightclub (allegedly) of more flesh-and-blood princes.

'Oh no!' sighed Jess stagily. 'I was so hoping to see him! I thought maybe I could pick up a bit of his dandruff – does that count as DNA? – then I could clone my very own prince back home on the window sill!'

The audience laughed some more, but then Jess saw, out of the corner of her eye, a white shape weaving its way through the tables, towards the stage. What on earth? She peered through the dark. Was it one of George's stupid jokes . . . ? No! Oh my God, thought Jess. A huge wave of panic crashed through her body.

It was Fred!

His head was poking out of a sheet on which streaks of green had been painted. What!? Fred sprang into the spotlight beside her and looked confidently out at the audience. Dave improvised a drum roll.

'My name,' announced Fred, 'is Prince Amoeba.' There was a laugh and a gust of applause. 'And though I don't have a backbone, I do at least have the presence of mind to welcome you all to this Valentine's event. Welcome, my friends, to Chaos!'

The band improvised a little riff of music, and the audience cheered and banged on the tables. Jess was furious. Fred had hijacked her routine! What was all this mad stuff about being an amoeba? She had no idea what Fred would say next – this was so off the wall. And how dare he put her in her place about welcoming people!

'I don't suppose many of you know much about amoebas,' Fred went on swiftly, so Jess didn't have a chance to open her mouth. 'I was discovered in 1757 by August Johann Rösel von Rosenhof. This was before the days of *Britain's Got Talent*, so unfortunately it didn't lead to a recording contract.'

There were cries of 'Shame!'

Jess could only stand there at his side, her mind simultaneously racing, reeling and somehow blank. She couldn't show her anger – she had to pretend this had all been planned. It was a nightmare.

'And I don't like to boast,' Fred continued, 'but I'm famous for my remarkably large genome.'

There was an explosion of laughing, and some guys at the back – possibly George and Co – hammered on the tables and howled.

'However,' Fred continued, 'I reproduce myself asexually, so any of you hoping to get lucky tonight are going to be disappointed.'

Presumably this amoeba stuff was what Fred had been working away at all week, all by himself on his goddam sofa. It must have been inspired by Jess calling him an invertebrate. How could she relate it to Cinderella? It was impossible. She just had to stand there like a dummy while Fred ranted selfishly on, stealing her limelight.

'In potentially lethal environments, such as a dinner dance,' said Fred, giving her the briefest glance, 'I roll into a ball and secrete a protective membrane around myself – in fact, I become a cyst.'

'Well, we all know that,' snapped Jess drily.

'I'm hoping to evolve into a higher life form,' Fred raced on, 'but it's still very much at the blueprint stage. It could take me, oh, three million years or so.' And suddenly, with a flourish, he disappeared from the stage.

Dave improvised another little drum roll, and there was a roar of applause, which should have given Jess a couple of seconds to collect her wits and work out what to say next.

There was a pause, and frantically she tried to remember the next bit of her script – although, would it make any sense after this amoeba garbage? To her horror, her mind went totally blank. There was nothing in her memory banks except a howling blackness. She went hot, then cold. For a moment she thought she was going to faint. The moment seemed to last for hours. Then, somehow, words came to her. She had to carry on where Fred had dumped the routine. Her Cinderella material seemed irrelevant now.

'Well, that's my little pet amoeba,' she said, her voice shaking slightly. 'He only consists of one cell, but hey! Who's counting?'

This got a slight titter, but nothing like the big laughs Fred had managed.

'Of course, I haven't got a ticket,' Jess went on, recovering her senses and remembering she had introducing to do, 'but I did overhear somebody backstage say that our DJ tonight is gorgeous Gordon Smith.' Another drum roll, a round of applause. 'And the band performing is The Martin Davies Undersextet! A buffet supper will be served at eight thirty by Polly Put The Kettle On and her team of wannabe Jamie Olivers!' There was clapping and cheering. 'But don't all rush – I'll tell you when it's time to grab your grub! Till then, enjoy yourselves. I must go off and defrost the chandeliers!'

Jess turned and ran backstage, hearing the comforting sound of the band striking up behind her. She headed for the sanctuary of her little dressing room, slammed the door behind her, slumped down in her chair, buried her head in her hands and shuddered. That terrible split second when her mind had gone blank! It was one of the worst moments of her entire life, and it was all Fred's fault. It was a good job he wasn't here – she might actually have hit him.

After a few minutes there was a knock on the door.

Jess whirled round in indignation, but it was only Mum with Ben Jones.

'You were brilliant, love!' said Mum. 'And trust Fred to take a really original approach!'

'Yes,' said Jess uneasily. She couldn't bear to reveal what had really happened: that Fred had ruined her routine, the evening and possibly her life.

'Is he going to be an amoeba all night?' asked Ben.

'Ah!' said Jess, heroically managing a tight little false smile. 'You'll just have to wait and see.'

The awful thing was that she would just have to wait and see, too. She couldn't go out and track Fred down for a showdown in front of everybody – all the guests had to think the double act was supposed to be like that. And clearly Fred's stupid amoeba idea had been a great hit. Jess remembered the applause he'd got – warmer, more excited applause than hers. She felt bitterly, bitterly betrayed and stupidly jealous.

Soon it was time for the buffet to be announced. Polly came round to Jess's dressing room and told her everything was ready. By now the bar was heaving, the joint was jumping and Dave had to roll his drums like a thunderstorm to get everyone to be quiet. Once again Jess stepped out into the spotlight. She glanced around. No sign of Fred. Then there were giggles from the back of the room, strange sounds, a kind of hurly-burly. Chairs were being moved about, and there was laughter and some good-natured hilarious screaming. Jess peered into the dark, inconveniently dazzled by the spotlight. Somebody in a monkey suit was rampaging around the tables. Oh God, what next?

It had to be Fred. He grabbed a woman and hauled her to her feet. Her hair came off – oh no, it was George Stevens, with a blonde wig and a red satin ball gown. He hoicked its straps back up on to his brawny rugby-player's shoulders, and screeched. The ape embraced him, then raced up to the stage.

'I see you've evolved a bit since we last met,' said Jess sourly, abandoning her Cinderella character and all its wonderful jokes.

'I wish I could say the same for you,' said Fred. He tilted the ape's head back so his own face was visible.

'I don't need to evolve,' Jess retorted. 'I'm perfect already.' She was managing to improvise, thank God, but it felt really lame compared to her lovely Cinderella script.

'Nobody's perfect!' Fred insisted. And there was a little *ta-tum* on the drums because that was a famous quote, the last line of the wonderful film *Some Like It*

Hot, which, annoyingly, was Jess and Fred's favourite movie.

'That's not what Prince Charming told me,' said Jess, trying desperately to reintroduce a vague hint of Cinderella. 'He came round to my dressing-room door with a bunch of red roses and a bottle of champagne just now, and asked me to be his valentine.' There were whoops of excitement from the crowd.

'Poor innocent child,' said Fred. 'You shouldn't let your head be turned by these Hooray Henrys. Place your trust in an ape – you know it makes sense.'

'But I can tell your affections are otherwise engaged,' said Jess crisply. 'I saw you flirting with that blonde lady at the back of the room.'

'That was no lady – that was my wife,' said Fred, leaning forward conspiratorially. Another *ta-tum* from the drums – Dave was very quick to respond whenever he heard a classic old joke.

'Anyway, ladies and gentlemen, it is now officially feeding time,' announced Jess. 'Please queue for the buffet at your convenience.'

'Funny place for a buffet,' commented Fred. 'Not very hygienic, I'd have thought. Well, folks, enjoy your supper. I'm off to guzzle a banana in my nest of leaves. I'm hoping to evolve into Homo sapiens by the end of the evening, but I can see that some of you have a lot further to go than that.' He threw this remark to the back of the hall, where George's table was. They raised a cheer, and people started to get up. Jess could see there was no need for her to say anything more, so she slipped back to her dressing room again, feeling desperate and defeated.

There was a knock on the door – it was Flora and Jack.

'Come out and have some supper, Jess!' suggested Flo. 'That buffet looks amazing – and you haven't got any more hosting to do till the end, have you?'

'No, I suppose not,' said Jess, wriggling back into her shoes. 'Is Fred out there?'

'Nobody knows where he is.' Flora shrugged. 'I thought *you* would know.'

'I expect he's festering in a swamp somewhere.' Jess tried to sound light-hearted rather than murderous – a challenge.

It was pandemonium out in the hall. The DJ was spinning his food music (as opposed to mood music) while the band had a break. People clutched at Jess as she passed, and hugged her and kissed her and told her how much they were enjoying themselves. She felt relieved as all the dread of the preceding weeks vanished – Chaos was a success. But her bitter fury at Fred's hijacking of her routine was still burning in her chest.

'Come to our table,' said Flora. 'We've got a chair for you.' Jess found herself sitting with George and Humph (both dragged up in wigs and ball gowns) and Tom, who looked completely normal in his tux and had a sweet girlfriend with long shiny hair and very pink cheeks.

'Jess, this is Rhiannon,' said Tom. 'And this is Lady MucRaker and her daughter – what's your name, mate?' he asked Humph.

'Susannah,' said Humph in a camp lisp.

'Great costumes,' commented Jess. 'It made me realise we should have specified fancy dress on the tickets.'

'This isn't fancy dress, child!' screeched George, looking down his nose at her. 'I'll have you know I rented this frock from Dame Viv herself!'

'Stunning!' Jess nodded.

'But tell me, dear.' George leaned across the table for a secret word. 'Are you engaged to that very distinguished ape? Because, if not, I'm tempted to have a crack at him myself. Such charisma!'

'Oh no, he's available,' Jess smiled. 'Although he

may have evolved into something else by now.' Suddenly she felt hungry, and she tucked into some chargrilled tuna with tabbouleh. Polly was right, it was delish.

Jess wasn't in the mood for dancing, so after the supper break she just sat and watched George and Humph fooling around. They both insisted on dancing with Jack (who looked embarrassed) and Tom (who looked as if nothing would embarrass him, ever). She tried to relax and enjoy herself. But she couldn't get past the monstrous injustice of what Fred had done to her. And because nobody must know, somehow she had to try and keep smiling. It was hard work – her face felt tired and twitchy.

Then, as the evening neared its end, Jess sneaked away backstage to get ready for her last appearance. This time she was introduced by Gordon the DJ.

'Ladies and gentlemen,' he cried, 'let's have a big hand for . . . Cinderella!'

Jess slid into the spotlight and curtsied to the crowd. There was clapping, cheering, stamping and whistling. When they had quietened down, she spoke.

'The organisers have asked me to read out this little message,' Jess said, fishing a crumpled piece of paper out of her corsage and smoothing it out. 'Oh dear, sorry, I forgot I can't read.' At this point she was supposed to interact with somebody in the audience and get them to read out a shopping list – pumpkins, mousetraps, firelighters, etc. – but once again her routine was swept aside.

Fred leapt into the spotlight, dressed as a naff Georgian prince with a powdered wig, white tights and buckled shoes. The tights looked ridiculous on his long skinny legs, and he struck up a ludicrous pose. The audience screamed with laughter as he tried to maintain his dignity. Fred turned on them with an indignant glare.

'As you can see, I've now evolved about as far up the food chain as I can possibly go,' he announced pompously.

'Bring back the amoeba!' shouted somebody at the back.

'At the last chime of midnight I shall *de*volve back into an amoeba, and not a moment sooner,' said Fred firmly. 'Until then, it only remains for me to thank you all for coming, and ask you to bear witness as I ask this ravishing creature if she will be my valentine!' Elaborately, he tottered down on one knee and held out his hand in a preposterous appeal to Jess.

Suddenly her mind went blank again as the howling blackness enveloped her. How dare he pitch her into this? She boiled with rage.

'I'm sorry,' she informed him icily, 'I can't be anyone's valentine right now. When the clock strikes midnight I shall turn back into a pumpkin – although some would say I've been a pumpkin all along! Goodnight, everybody, and thanks for coming!' She turned and ran offstage, then paused in the wings to listen – Fred was saying something else.

'What?' he cried theatrically. 'No glass slipper? Not even a dropped contact lens? Who was she? She's gone! And I don't even know her name!'

'It was Jess Jordan!' shouted somebody.

'No, no, that beautiful stranger couldn't be Jess Jordan. I haven't met Jess Jordan but I hear she's one of the ugly sisters.' Fred glanced briefly into the wings, where Jess was standing, and winked. It was obviously meant to be a joke, but in Jess's present state of mind she received it as a slap in the face. 'Well,' he went on, 'whoever that ravishing creature was, I shall spend the rest of my life searching for her, and until I find her, no other woman will turn my head for a moment. Although if any of you ladies would like to kiss my shoe buckle, you're welcome to form a queue. Thank you for coming, and goodnight!'

A midnight-style blast of music, complete with chimes, rang out. Jess, peeping from the wings, saw Fred vanish in the direction of the bar, and the whole hall was swamped with cheering. The awfulness of the past few weeks with Fred, culminating in him literally stealing what should have been her comedy triumph, overwhelmed Jess, and she darted back to her dressing room, fighting back tears of absolute rage.

Chapter 34

Moments later, Flora arrived with Jack. She threw herself into Jess's arms and gave her the biggest hug ever.

'You were brilliant!' she yelled. 'It was terrific! The whole evening really rocked! Come out and meet your public!'

Jess realised that she had to go out because, apart from anything else, she hadn't thanked all the people who had helped her: Mum and Dad, Martin and Polly, Ben Jones and his cousin Melissa . . . She should really have thanked them in her farewell speech, but her farewell speech had been brushed aside by Fred's relentless egotism.

People were leaving, waving and calling goodbye to one another, the hall was emptying, and Dad was already up a ladder fiddling with some lights. Jess found Polly and all her mates – they'd cleared the buffet away long ago and were chilling out, sitting along the edge of the stage.

'Thanks so much!' Jess told them. 'The buffet was just amazingly delicious, and it all went like clock-work!'

'Our pleasure!' said Polly. 'Any time you're holding another event, just let us know!'

'Sure!' said Jess, though privately she had promised herself that she would never organise another event as long as she lived. Then Martin appeared. 'Thanks so much, Martin – the band was terrific!' cried Jess, giving him a grateful hug. She really hoped that Martin would be around in her life from now on, but it all depended on Mum really. And on Dad, currently only visible from the knees down as he was up a ladder, fiddling with some lights.

'The lighting was amazing,' murmured Flora with a sigh. 'That mirror ball! And all those lasers! It was just stunning!'

Jess looked around the thinning crowds for Fred. She had to confront him – she was seething. Maybe he would be helping his dad.

'I have to thank Fred's dad for running the bar,' she said. 'I won't be a minute!'

She went off to the side room, where Mr Parsons was packing glasses away in a box.

'Thanks so much for running the bar, Mr Parsons!' Jess gushed. 'You were absolutely wonderful!'

'I'll have their guts for garters, never fear,' he replied with his usual charismatic gloominess. She supposed this must refer to Frobisher's Filthy Glasses Ltd.

'Is Fred not here? I thought he'd be helping you?' she asked.

Mr Parsons shrugged. 'He could be anywhere,' he said with a melancholy sigh, as if Fred was regularly glimpsed on the ceiling, up the chimney, or hanging from the minute hand of the town-hall clock.

'Well, thanks so much for helping out,' she blustered, moving towards the door. Mr Parsons was so weird. Still, he had run the bar for them. This was the longest conversation she had ever had with him, and she was going to keep things like that.

Back in the hall, there were now only a few groups of people laughing and gathering their things together. No Fred. Jess smiled falsely to the last few departing friends while blazing with hidden fury. Fred couldn't just go home and pretend that that was it, everything was sorted. How dare he?

If she couldn't find him, she'd have to phone him when she got home and tell him just what a stupid, thoughtless, destructive thing he'd done. First, though, she had to get her coat – now the hall was emptying, she could feel cold air sneaking in from the lobby. She shivered and went backstage to her dressing room again.

There was Fred, coming out of it! He looked startled and embarrassed.

'Oh,' he said. 'I was just leaving you a note.'

'A note?' Somehow the idea of a note filled Jess with even more indignation. She dragged Fred into the dressing room and shut the door. 'Couldn't face me, huh?' she demanded.

Fred cringed. 'No, no,' he stammered. 'It's just – I've got to go now – I think my flu has come back. I shouldn't really have come out tonight.'

'You bet you shouldn't have come out tonight!' yelled Jess. 'Have you any idea what you've just done?'

For an instant Fred looked genuinely stunned and puzzled. 'Done?' he asked dumbly.

'You ruined my routine!' cried Jess. 'I'd worked out this really brilliant, brilliant routine, all about

Cinderella – I've been working on it all week, at the same time, may I remind you, as having to organise this whole event! OK, I turn up, really looking forward to the hosting bit, and you just come barging in and upstage me in front of everybody!'

'But . . .' Fred's lip trembled. In the harsh light of the dressing room, Jess could see beads of sweat breaking out across his brow. 'I thought you'd be pleased that I turned up and gave you some support.'

'*Support?*' screamed Jess. '*Pleased?* Pleased that you hijacked the whole goddam evening and didn't let me get a word in? Pleased that I worked for hours polishing great gags that I never got a chance to deliver? Pleased that I didn't have a clue what you were going to say next? Pleased I had to improvise, and that I was lame and stupid when I actually managed to get a word in, which was almost never?! I was so freakin' pleased with the whole situation that when you bounded off the stage and disappeared after your goddam amoeba thing, I completely dried up! My mind was a total blank! My ears were horrible and roaring and I thought I was going to faint! If that's what you call support, you can keep it!'

'Phew!' said Fred after a pause, wiping his brow. 'I

think I might be going to faint myself.'

'Go home, then!' hissed Jess, incredulous and seething because he still didn't seem to realise what he'd done. Instead of apologising, he had grabbed the limelight yet again – he was going to faint now, and his faintingness was going to be so much more important than hers! 'Go home and go to bed.' She glared defiantly at him.

He hesitated in his gangling way, which she had so often found adorable. But not now. Now it was infuriating.

'Yes, I'll be off,' said Fred. 'I'll see you – sometime.' And he turned round and went away, shutting the door behind him.

Jess began to shake and shiver. Her mind was reeling from the row. This was the worst that things had ever been between them. She reached for her coat and scarf. Then she noticed there was an envelope propped against the mirror – Fred's note! Her heart lurched. She stopped for a moment. Looking down at her own hands holding the envelope, she noticed her fingers trembling like mad. It was irritating to be so upset. She ripped the envelope open and inside was a folded piece of paper. On one side were lines she recognised from his amoeba routine, with a lot of crossings-out and added scribbles. He'd drawn a big line across those. She turned over. On the other side were the words he'd written to her:

Jess, you're a bit of a legend to have organised all this. Your Cinderella thing was hilarious. Sorry I have been so totally useless all along. Thank you for refraining from strangling me – it's these little courtesies that make life worth living. See you around – if you can spare the time for a fleeting glance at an invertebrate. Fred.

A riot of conflicting emotions flooded Jess's heart. What was he hoping to achieve by this? To wheedle his way back into her affections? It was an apology, sure, but it wasn't an apology for stealing her comedy evening – the worst thing he had ever done. He hadn't seemed to realise how selfish he'd been. He'd enjoyed all the applause – applause which ought to have been hers.

OK, he'd praised her organisational skills and her stand-up routine had been 'hilarious'. But she hadn't had a chance to deliver the most hilarious bits. They'd been swept aside by his confident hogging of the limelight. Was it bad of her to feel so resentful? She couldn't help it. She sat down on the hard, cheap little chair and stared at herself in the mirror. Her mascara was slightly smudged from her previous brush with tearfulness. Her cheeks were flushed. Her eyes were bright, but not in a good way. She looked like somebody who had escaped from a fire, shocked and scorched.

She found a big sigh waiting in her ribcage and let it out. She took her earrings off – she didn't like their sparkle. She looked at her hands – they had stopped trembling. If only Fred had stayed at home with the flu! She would have had a wonderful success, and their relationship . . . well, they might have salvaged it. But now, she felt something truly awful – hatred. Hatred, for Fred? Impossible. Well, anger, perhaps.

She tore Fred's note up and threw it in the bin. A fragment of it missed and fell on the floor. She scooped it up: *if you can spare the time for a fleeting glance at an invertebrate*. Then she decided what she was going to do. It just wasn't acceptable for Fred to behave like this. To get back into her good books, he was going to have to change.

Like somebody in a fairytale, he was going to have to earn her respect all over again – from the beginning. If indeed he could be bothered. And if he couldn't be bothered, so what? There were plenty more fish in the sea.

Jess sighed again, but this time with a faint sense of relief. She felt as if she had got control of herself again at last. She didn't look too bad for a girl who had just been through a nervous breakdown and needed about three days' sleep.

Somebody appeared in the mirror behind her. It was Mum.

'Hi, love,' she said softly. 'Well done! The whole thing was a spectacular success. I haven't done all the sums yet but it looks as if you've made hundreds of pounds for Oxfam!'

'Oh, brilliant!' said Jess, cheerful to be thinking about something mega important, not her own little on-off love affair.

'Did you see Fred?' asked Mum. 'Are things OK between you two now?'

'So-so,' said Jess, getting up and reaching for her coat. 'But that's OK. Give it time.' She couldn't face telling Mum all about it now.

'The band was great, wasn't it?'

'Yes!' said Jess. 'Thanks so much for helping me out, Mum. If it hadn't been for you and Dad and Martin, I'd have had to cancel the whole thing.'

'The food was great, too,' said Mum. 'I suppose if

I hadn't had a dodgy date or two we'd never have met Polly.'

'Right!' agreed Jess. 'Tell you what, Mum, let's have a big Sunday lunch tomorrow and invite Martin, shall we?'

'I don't know . . .' Mum hesitated. 'Martin won't be able to come – he's flying out to Canada on Monday for some kind of showdown with his ex-wife.'

'Oh?' Jess was immediately concerned. She hadn't even known that he had an ex-wife. Was it really a showdown, or could it turn into a reconciliation? 'Men! Aren't they useless?' She sighed, and took Mum's arm as they walked out into the hall. It was empty now apart from Dad, who was standing in the middle of the floor, winding a length of cable round his arm. He looked tired. 'Not counting Dad, of course,' she added affectionately.

Jess ran up and gave him a hug. 'Thanks for the awesome lighting, Dad!' she said. 'It was utterly amazing!'

'I'll have to spend all tomorrow dismantling it and taking it back to Oxford,' said Dad. 'Jack and his brother said they'd help me, thank God. Really nice guys, those boys.'

Jess was silent, aware that for Fred to be unavailable with tragic flu only emphasised the difference between him and the Jackass gang. In some sense Fred wasn't really 'a normal bloke'. Even if he hadn't been ill and he had tried to help dismantle the lights, he'd almost certainly have ended up breaking something. Fred always ended up breaking things . . . Jess didn't want to take that thought any further.

'And then, next week,' announced Dad, 'I start to look for a job and somewhere to live.'

'So we've all got projects,' said Jess thoughtfully.

'What's yours, love?' asked Mum, taking her arm again.

'I'll tell you when we get home,' said Jess.

She wasn't sure if she would, though. Her ongoing melodrama with Fred was something she didn't really fancy talking about. But in a way she was quite looking forward to it – it was a strange new adventure and Jess couldn't wait for the next act to unfold.

Are you now Jess Jordan's #1 fan?
Read on and meet the equally hilarious duo
Zoe and Chloe in

Girls, Guilty But Somehow Glorious
by Sue Limb

Zoe and Chloe. Chloe and Zoe. Best friends together.
Until Chloe falls under the spell of the darkly
dangerous 'Beast' Hawkins . . .

FRIDAY 1.45 P.M.

Seven days to the earthquake . . .

'We could always . . . just not go,' I said. We were crossing the schoolyard at change of lessons.

'Not *go*???' cried Chloe. 'Not *GO*? Zoe!'

'I only thought . . .' I said, offering her a piece of my chewing gum, 'we could maybe just kind of ignore it. I mean, stay in and watch the football, or something.'

Zoe scowled. 'But what about all those poor homeless earthquake victims?' she demanded. 'The Earthquake Ball's not just for fun, it's to raise money, yeah? Besides, I hate football! *Hate it!*'

Hmm. It had been a mistake to mention football. I quite like a spot of footie, myself. I enjoy watching England losing gallantly. I might even paint the St George's flag on my face, one day. It would hide the spots – especially the massive zit which keeps resurfacing again and again on my chin (I call it Nigel).

But Chloe's not into football. In fact, she's not really much into any kind of sport. If you throw her a ball, somehow it tends to hit her on the nose, and if you force her into a pool, she swims like a mad little dog in a panic.

'OK, not football, sorry,' I said. 'But maybe a DVD?'

'Oh nooooo!' wailed Chloe. 'We *can't* miss the Earthquake Ball! The Ball is gonna be where it's at! Think of the music! The noise! The headaches! The vomiting! The jealousy! The fights! The broken hearts!' Her face had a wistful, faraway look. In her imagination, she was already *there*.

'OK, then,' I said. 'Yeah, let's go – I was just being stupid.' I shrugged amiably. One of us has to be chilled out, and clearly, Chloe could never play that vital role.

'Yes,' said Chloe. 'We're going. That's obvious. *Obvious!* But here's the major prob: who's going to take us?'

I tossed another piece of gum into my mouth. It's amazing how quickly it loses its charm. I offered a piece to Chloe.

'No!' said Chloe. 'My brace, remember?'

'Sorry, sorry,' I said. Chloe's brace had been such an epic ordeal. 'Does it hurt at the moment?' I asked.

'No, but I've got to have it adjusted in a couple of

weeks' time. I'd rather do maths for the *rest of my life* than have my brace adjusted *for even two minutes*.'

She looked anxious. Maths is one of her very worst ordeals. Or, as she might put it: 'Maths is two of my very worst ordeals.'

Chloe sighed, and snuggled more deeply into her fleece. Though fresh, the air was also almost freezing. We plunged through the swing doors into the warmth of the corridor.

'Who in the world is going to take us to the Ball, though?' said Chloe miserably. 'If we can't find a couple of boys to go with, we'll be social rejects.'

'What about Fergus and Toby?' I pondered. 'They'd probably take us. If we paid them.'

'Fergus and Toby?' screeched Chloe in horror. 'Nothing personal, I mean they're great guys . . .' she looked round furtively, to make sure neither Fergus nor Toby had inconveniently appeared. 'I would rather walk down the high street wearing *only* an old man's trilby hat than go with either Fergus or Toby.'

'What's wrong with them?' I asked. I quite like Fergus and Toby. They're in our class and they're a laugh.

'Zoe, they're so immature, they're practically foetuses!' whispered Chloe. 'I mean, Fergus is a microbe!'

'I think you may be exaggerating just a tad,' I said, laughing. 'He perched on my hand to peck up a few crumbs yesterday and he was definitely heavier than the average microbe.'

'Fergus is approximately five centimetres high,' insisted Chloe. 'And Toby is technically a cream bun. I mean, we're talking serious lard here.'

'Harsh,' I objected. 'Toby's cuddly. Not that I want to cuddle him – no, no! I'd rather cuddle your dog.'

'Zoe,' said Chloe, putting on her mock headmistress voice, 'dogs are not allowed at the Earthquake Ball. You cannot go to the Ball with Geraint as your escort. People would talk.'

I laughed, but the problem remained. Why did everything have to be so difficult?

Then – oh God! – the swing doors at the far end of the corridor opened, and somebody walked towards us. Oliver Wyatt! Oliver tall-dark-and-haunted-looking Wyatt! Ashcroft School's answer to Heathcliff. I instantly forgot all about the Earthquake Ball.

My Heights Wuthered. My heart turned into a caged jaguar. A firework display went off in my chest. Whole flocks of butterflies flew out of my ears.

'We *can't* go with anybody from our year,' Chloe said. She looked thoughtful. She hadn't noticed Oliver. *Hadn't noticed.* She was ransacking her bag.

'Hmmm,' I said. The god was strolling towards us. He was a mere metre away. I didn't look at him, of course. I looked at the floor. I knew every detail of his appearance by heart anyway. He didn't stop. He didn't speak to us. He was totally unaware of my spotty, sad, nerdy little life.

I noticed a tiny patch of mud on the side of his right shoe. What wouldn't I give to be that tiny patch of mud! The air stirred up by him swirled around me. There was a faint smell of limes. (His aftershave, obviously: he isn't a greengrocer.) I inhaled deeply, hoping to capture that divine scent for ever.

'We have to corner somebody in the sixth form,' said Chloe. 'They've got to be sixteen or over. I'm too young for a toyboy. Ah, there's my phone. I thought I'd lost it again.' She turned to me and frowned. 'What's up?'

'Oliver Wyatt just walked past!' I whispered. Chloe's eyes flared excitedly. She turned round. She was just in time to see his back disappearing through some swing doors.

'God! Sorry I missed the sacred moment!' She grinned. 'Did he throw you a contemptuous look of burning passion?'

'Certainly,' I informed her. 'But I'm not quite sure whether it's me he loves, or Nigel.' I fingered my chin anxiously. I could feel Nigel lurking there. He'd gone to ground for the past couple of days, but I could sense he was planning to erupt again, possibly on the left-hand side. If one must have a Nobel-prize-winning zit, it at least should be central. For absolute zit perfection, symmetry is essential.

'Have you seen Jack yet today?' I asked. Chloe has a major crush on Jack Bennett, this wicked guy who can break-dance on his head – and let's face it, what else could one possibly ask of a potential husband?

'I don't know . . .' pondered Chloe. 'I haven't felt quite the same about him since I saw him peeing in that alley after the Cramp gig.' Chloe's so easily put off. She can fall madly for somebody at lunchtime and find them loathsome by nightfall. I wouldn't be put off if I saw Oliver peeing. I know he'd pee in a divine, stylish way which would turn it almost into an art form.

'OK,' I said, reluctantly abandoning thoughts of Oliver, 'let's get started.' We had to find a couple of fit partners for the Ball.

'Right, then,' sighed Chloe. 'Where *do* we start?' She offered me a piece of chocolate. I accepted. I think it's good for the brain.

'We start by drawing up a shortlist.'

The bell rang. My heart sank. It was time for

German. I don't object to Germany or the Germans at all in principle, it's just that for the first few lessons, when we were starting out, I didn't pay attention. I am a bit of a dreamer, I admit it.

And when, after a couple of months, I sort of woke up and started to concentrate, it was too late. The rest of the class were deep in the book *Das geheimnisvolle Dorf* and stuff like that and I knew that the moment had passed and I would never, never, be able to speak a word of German apart from one rather special one. I could more easily communicate with Chloe's dog, Geraint – by barking.

'OK,' said Chloe, 'let's make the list in German.'

I groaned. 'God, no!' I begged. 'Please, not in German! I just can't cope with it.'

'I didn't mean we were going to make the list in German, Zoe,' giggled Chloe. 'I meant we're going to make the list in *German*!'

OUT NOW

Fred and Jess star in another hilarious
story, involving Gallic passion, muddy
tents and aggressive cows!

Out Now!